The SKY Beneath the STONE

ALEX MULLARKY

ROYAL BOROUGH OF GREENWICH

Follow us on twitter 🐦 @greenwichlibs

Please return by the last date shown		
— JUN 2023		
1 4 AUG 2023		
1 4 AUG 2023		
Thank you! To renew, please contact any Royal Greenwich library or renew online or by phone www.better.org.uk/greenwichlibraries 24hr renewal line 01527 852385		

For my Grendel,
who has gone through the wall

Kelpies is an imprint of Floris Books
First published in 2022 by Floris Books
© 2022 Alex Mullarky

Author photo courtesy of Mairhi MacLeod
Map © 2022 Floris Books

 Also available as an eBook

British Library CIP data available
ISBN 978-178250-787-1
Printed & bound by MBM Print SCS Ltd, Glasgow

 Floris Books supports sustainable forest management by
printing this book on materials made from wood that
comes from responsible sources and reclaimed material

MIX
Paper from
responsible sources
FSC® C117931

Praise for *The Sky Beneath the Stone*

"I absolutely adored this! *The Sky Beneath the Stone* is beautiful, bright and brilliant – a perfect blend of magic, adventure and heart, with a gorgeous Cumbrian setting, a wonderful weaving of nature, folklore and history, heart-lifting incidental inclusivity, and OS grid references at the start of each chapter so you can map the journey! It is one of those books I want to press into every young reader's hands, because I know so many of them will fall in love with it."

– Sophie Anderson, Carnegie-shortlisted author of *The House with Chicken Legs*

"A beautifully written adventure steeped in the myths and magic of the Lake District. I long to journey through the wall and explore the enchanted, dangerous wilds of Underfell!"

– Ross MacKenzie, author of the *Nowhere Emporium* trilogy

A Note

*At the beginning of each chapter is an
Ordnance Survey grid reference.*

*Adventurous souls can find their way
around this story using Ordnance Survey
maps of the United Kingdom.*

The Goshawk

OS Grid Ref: NY 17 00

First: the map. Ivy smoothed it out over the ground, pressed a finger to her location and circled it with a pencil. It wasn't her preferred campsite, but it would have to do. She timed herself as she slotted her tent poles together and raised the heap of fabric into a shelter. Her record was four minutes, but she did it in five. That was disappointing; she was getting rusty.

She dug out her sleeping bag and mat and set up her bed, hanging the lantern overhead for when darkness fell. If the weather turned, she'd still be warm and cosy inside. At a safe distance from the shelter, she took out her dinner supplies and assembled the stove, though she didn't light it since her mum had asked her to stop doing that here.

When everything was ready, she grabbed the map again and crawled into the quiet blue cocoon of the tent. Her socked feet rustled against the sleeping bag as she took out her pencil and traced a route to Harter Fell. A day's walk, probably, and there was a barn where she could shelter if a storm blew in.

She squeezed out of the tent again and pulled her binoculars from her pack, squinting through them at the fields in the distance. The window frame was obscuring her view, as usual.

"IVY!"

Callum's voice echoed in the hallway. She could already hear his footsteps thundering up the staircase to her room. A moment later, the door flew open.

"Last day of school!" Callum stood panting in the doorway. His brown eyes sparkled beneath his heavy eyebrows, scanning the tent, the carpet, the window. His mouth quirked in its habitual lopsided smile. Ivy's little brother was tall for his nine years, and lean because some part of him was always in motion.

Ivy peered around the corner of the tent, which took up most of the floor of her room.

"Good morning to you, too."

"Mum says it's time to go!"

Ivy checked her watch and balked. She let the worn map accordion back into its deep folds and tucked it into her blazer pocket.

"Which one have you got today?" she asked Callum as they descended both flights of stairs together. He opened one of his hands so that Ivy could see. A piece of yolk-golden citrine, rubbed almost smooth from years of being rolled around in Callum's palms.

At the front door they pulled on their shoes and called goodbye to their mum. Iona's porcelain face appeared around her studio door; her eyes, on Ivy, were gentle and questioning.

"I can drive you," she offered for the hundredth time.

Ivy felt the immediate, desperate urge to say, *Yes, okay.* Instead she said, "No, I can do it."

Only one more day until the summer holidays. All she had to do was get there.

Before she stepped outside, Ivy slipped the map out of her pocket and opened it to the folds that depicted their house and the surrounding village. Her eyes followed the smudged pencil line that traced the route from home to school.

Callum was watching her, and when she raised her head he set off. Ivy squinted as she stepped into the sunlight after him, pushing down the tremor of nausea that surged up her throat. She kept her head down, placing one foot in front of the other.

As she walked, her thoughts kept returning to the six empty weeks ahead of her and the route she had plotted that morning. How much she would love to follow that path to Harter Fell – and then keep going, climb every fell in the county, ramble around every lake, cross every valley. No school, nothing but time and the freedom to explore with Callum and her mum.

But then she remembered the well-worn map in her hands, and she felt herself deflate like a popped balloon. She tucked it away.

It had been a year now. A year since she'd gotten herself lost in the fells, a year since she'd become too scared to step out of the front door without the security of her map. Even then, she couldn't walk anywhere she hadn't gone a hundred times before.

This was going to be a very long, very boring summer.

The sky was so blue and vast overhead, almost cloudless. Ivy shrank away from it, her eyes fixed on the tarmac starting to glisten in the heat.

She went over the exercises the psychologist had taught her to keep her mind still. She focused on her chest, rising and falling with each breath. The weight of her body as she set one foot in front of the other, dodging piles of sheep poo and dandelions popping up at the edge of the single-track road.

Callum was speeding ahead, but he stopped to run his hands over a drystone wall. A blackbird sang in the hedge as they turned down the familiar lonning towards school.

A series of shrill cries punctured the morning stillness. Ivy stopped in her tracks, her ears pricking.

She scanned the sky without thinking. Callum pointed to the treeline and said, "There!"

The bird soared in a couple of slow circles, and as it turned side-on Ivy saw the speckled markings of its feathers, the straight line of its tail.

"Goshawk!" they called at the same time.

Callum set off running. Ivy was right behind him, and she followed him over the wooden gate and into the pasture where dairy cows grazed obliviously around them. A goshawk! They had never seen one so close to home before.

"Watch out!" Callum called as Ivy was almost bowled over by a blur of black-and-white. A great pink tongue lunged for her face, and she turned away to avoid the onslaught.

"Down, Grendel!" she laughed as his paws printed dirt all over her school uniform.

"Where have you been this morning?" she asked him as he grinned up at her, panting. He wasn't their dog; nobody seemed quite sure who he belonged to. Nevertheless, he was well fed and well loved by the villagers of Beckfoot. He often jumped the gate into their garden to play with Callum.

But Callum wasn't to be distracted today – he was at the opposite hedge already. "It's gone into the next field," he called back to Ivy, and without further ado, he climbed through a gap in the blackthorn, swiftly followed by Grendel.

Ivy felt a little flutter in her chest, but she took a breath and set off after them.

She heard the goshawk's call again as she pulled herself through the hedge. The field she found herself in was a sea of long grasses and wildflowers. The ground sloped away from them in all directions, layers of fells stretching off into the distance, and suddenly Ivy felt dizzily as though she was standing on the edge of the sky.

The world began to grow grey and blurry. Callum laughed, turning on the spot as he followed the shape of the goshawk's flight from below. The outline of the gliding bird flickered as Ivy's vision swam, and then she stopped seeing it all together. There was only the sky, vast and heavy.

Her gaze fell at last to her feet and the grass beneath them.

She had gone off the path.

Her breath came in fast gulps. She scrabbled to pull the map from her pocket, but her fingers didn't seem to be obeying her commands.

This was the land she had grown up in, lakes and mountains that were as familiar as her own family. But for the past year they had felt like strangers to her, as jarring as looking into a mirror one day and not recognising your own face. The fells she had once seen as gentle and rolling were now uncertain and menacing, a landscape waiting to swallow her whole.

A grey fog was clouding her vision, muffling the sounds in her ears. *Focus on your breathing*, she told herself, but she couldn't turn the thought into action.

She sank to the ground, pressing her forehead into the grass, her knees tucked in against her chest. Her mind was too loud to separate her thoughts.

Callum was gently rocking her shoulder, but it was like trying to uncurl a frightened hedgehog. She couldn't move. Grendel was whining and licking beseechingly at her hands, and she couldn't even bat him away.

The sound of Callum's voice reached her as though through a closed window. Grass tickled her face as tears leaked from her tightly shut eyes onto the dirt.

By the time the fog had cleared, Ivy was sitting in the threadbare armchair in Iona's studio, a cup of hot chocolate in her hands. The curtains were drawn and she was alone, though she didn't think she had been for long. There was scuffling in the hallway, and Ivy overheard Callum's voice, quick and distressed.

"I couldn't even get her to look at me – Grendel was worried and I was getting *really* worried – and when she stood up she was like a zombie, she didn't even look where she was going! How is she ever going to be able to go anywhere ever again—"

"Hey," their mum interrupted gently. Her voice was low and soothing, clearly not intended for Ivy to hear. "Listen to me. Your sister used to be fearless, like you. But fear is a helpful thing sometimes. It keeps us out of danger. Ivy got a fright, but it won't last forever. In the end it will make her stronger, when she's far enough away to look back at it clearly." There was a pause. "Come on – we'd better give the school a ring."

Their footsteps moved away into the kitchen. Ivy's face was hot and there was an ache in her wrists and hands that was almost unbearable. She took a few tentative sips of her hot chocolate and focused on slowing her breathing.

The studio was like a cocoon, warmed by the heat of the kiln. The blue-grey walls were hung with charcoal drawings of birds and animals, underscored by bookshelves full of old hardback books with titles printed in silver and gold. Iona didn't really care what they were about; she was in love with musty cloth-bound books and never came out of a second-hand bookshop without one.

The door creaked open and Iona appeared, bearing a packet of chocolate biscuits. When Ivy met her eyes, her mum smiled with relief, popped a biscuit out of the packet for herself and handed the rest to Ivy. Iona sat down at her potter's wheel, set her foot to the pedal and went on with her work.

"Callum tells me you went all the way to Ewan's field." Her hands gently persuaded a lump of wet grey clay into the rough shape of a plate.

Ivy felt her heart speed up, the palest memory of her panic attack. "We don't need to talk about it," she replied, circling her hands around her mug.

"We should." Iona focused on the almost-plate. "Your brother did well to get you home."

"He's not the one you have to worry about." Heat rushed to Ivy's cheeks.

"No. He's not," Iona agreed, and when Ivy looked up she found her mum looking right at her, her green eyes bright. "It's never a straight road," she said. "It'll take as long as it takes."

Somehow hearing that made her feel worse. "I know," Ivy said glumly. She took a few biscuits from the packet. "I think I'll go back to bed."

Back in her room Ivy crept into the safe blue dome of her tent. She dug out one of her dog-eared walking guides and tried to cheer herself up by planning a walk she would take with Callum and Iona and maybe Grendel, just as soon as everything was back to normal.

If it ever was.

The Hole in the Wall

OS Grid Ref: NY 17 00

Ivy woke up on the first morning of the school holidays to the warmth of the sun on her face and a chorus of song thrushes and blackbirds outside her window. After a whole day and night spent in bed her body felt like a coiled spring, and she propelled herself up out of bed as though she were one.

When she reached the foot of the stairs she could hear the whir of her mum's wheel through the studio door. She padded past to the kitchen, where she ate a bowl of cereal beside the window overlooking the veggie garden.

It was already late, she realised when she glanced at the clock. She had slept most of the morning away.

She never took the map into the garden with her; she had been treading this patch of ground her whole life. The garden was really just an extension of the sanctuary offered by the four walls of their tilting blue-slate house.

When she stepped outside the air was crisp and fresh and filled with birdsong, the grass rubbery and cool beneath her bare feet. But Callum was nowhere to be found. Not in the boulder field, where they had brought in the biggest stones they could find in the wheelbarrow and spaced them apart like a stone circle; nor the rock pool, where Callum's favourite pebbles from the beck were kept gleaming beneath shallow water. He wasn't lying on his back in the wildflower meadow. Nor was he building another cairn along the top of the drystone wall.

Ivy pushed open the studio door and stepped onto the smooth flagstone floor. Her mum was elbow-deep in what looked like an enormous plant pot.

"Have you seen Callum?" Ivy asked. She noticed a wet pot seeping into a book and swooped in to rescue them both.

"He'll be in the garden somewhere," Iona said breezily.

"He isn't," Ivy protested. The three of them were a unit: Iona and Callum and Ivy. Each always knew where the others would be.

Iona's shoulders shook in a little laugh. "The two of you worry about each other more than I do. I think you forget who the parent is sometimes."

Ivy narrowed her eyes sceptically but decided not to engage her mum on that front. If they hadn't heard from Callum for this long there was bound to be a reason.

She checked his bedroom. The windowsill, the mantelpiece, the bookshelves and the headboard of the bed were all lined with jars of pebbles, categorised by size, colour and shape. On the walls were posters depicting the geological eras of the British Isles and the differences between igneous, sedimentary and metamorphic rocks. Unlike his mum and sister, Callum kept his room meticulously organised. The only item out of place was a green book lying closed on his pillow.

Fighting a rising tide of panic, Ivy went back to her room and sat down at the window, chewing the inside of her cheek.

There was a flash of movement in the corner of her eye. Grendel! He was pacing up and down a stretch of wall at the far end of the garden. It occurred to her that there was a chance, if a small one, that Grendel might be able to lead her to Callum.

Ivy rushed down the stairs and out the front door, twigs and stones poking into the tender soles of her feet as she crossed the grass. She called to Grendel as she approached, but though he wagged his tail low and slow he didn't come to her, and as she drew closer, she realised why.

There was a hole in the wall. A hole that had never been there before.

Grendel was fixated on it, sniffing around its edge and whining. Ivy was not quite sure how a hole could have appeared in their garden wall, given that the drystone structure was an intricate puzzle. Even if Callum had been experimenting with pulling stones out, he couldn't have created such a perfect gap at ground level. You'd have to be a master stonemason.

Ivy felt a prickling sensation travel up her neck and behind her ears.

Then Grendel's eyes fixed on something through the hole, and he barked, which made her jump – that wasn't like him. She shielded her eyes against the sky and looked out across the fields beyond the garden, but there was nothing – no one – there.

"Callum?"

There was no response, no movement. Only the long grass swaying in the breeze.

With a sinking sensation, Ivy realised it was time to tell Iona that Callum had vanished. She took two steps away – and then she heard his voice.

"IVY!" It sounded distant – and desperate. "Ivy!"

"Callum?" She wheeled around. He was nowhere in sight.

"Ivy!" came his voice again, and Grendel barked twice at the hole in the wall. Her brow creasing in confusion, Ivy knelt down to Grendel's level and looked through the opening.

She nearly toppled backwards when she saw Callum running towards her. He was sprinting across the field towards the garden, toiling up the slope but still running as fast as she'd ever seen him. She scrambled back to her feet, but the second she straightened up and looked over the wall, he was gone.

"Ivy, here!" Callum yelled frantically.

The sound was coming from the hole in the wall.

She dropped to her knees again, peering through the gap between the stones, and though her mind rebelled against what she saw, there he was in the field again.

There was something wrong about the colours of the sky and the fells in the distance. Callum was running for his life, tripping and stumbling and shaking his head.

"Are you okay?!" she shouted. He was still a hundred metres away at least. He drew nearer, and her stomach dropped as she realised that he was engulfed in a swarm of small birds. They were darting around him and pecking at his clothes and hair, doing everything they could to get in his way.

"Come here!" Callum's arm was outstretched, hand curled into a fist.

Ivy felt a thrum of panic.

She shook her head. She couldn't.

But what was that sound? The air seemed to be full of a low rumbling – a voice. It was a song, though she couldn't understand the words, and it was issuing like a blast of wind from the hole itself. Callum was trying to cover his ears with his hands, and she recognised the signs that his words were wisping away.

He was close now, and she saw the bright autumnal colours of the little finches that harassed him as he ran. Something about the song was urgent and frightening in a way that Ivy didn't understand. Callum looked at her. Straight at her, right into her eyes. He couldn't speak, but that gesture communicated everything. He needed her. She *had* to go to him.

She straightened up again, preparing herself to jump over the wall and run to his aid. But – he wasn't there!

She dropped back down, shaking her head, and there he was.

Through the wall.

Not in the field on the other side of it.

In a different place entirely.

The song was growing louder and louder and something about Callum's run was wrong now, too. He was hobbling, one shoulder jerking back as if being pulled by a string. His eyes went wide in alarm.

Now her breath was coming fast. Ivy put her hands on the stones on either side of the hole to pull herself through, but her searching gaze found no sign of a path. A grey fog pushed in around the edges of her vision and blurred everything. She let go.

Callum's eyes found hers again, pleading with her to come. Misery gripped her and she tried to move again but her body resisted – she didn't have her map; she didn't know the way!

Callum stumbled. Something was wrapped around his legs. They weren't his legs any more. His left arm was not an arm; it had become a wing, and his right was stretched out to her.

The deep, resonant singing filled her ears, a chant that echoed in the fells.

Callum was almost upon her, and she screwed up her face and shoved her arm through the hole in the wall, grasping for his hand, and found it. Something smooth and small was pressed into her palm, and the hand that had held it became soft like down and slipped out of her reach.

Ivy opened her eyes, fingers closing on nothing but that small object, just in time to see the last of Callum swallowed up into—

A bird.

A bird that winged up and away from her, chittering shrilly, its wingbeats uncoordinated and frantic. The flock of finches swarmed upon it and drove it high into that strange sky, and then it was gone.

The singing abruptly ceased. The weight of the sky settled onto Ivy and she scrambled back from the hole, heart racing. Grendel was at her side, licking and nudging her and whining in agitation.

Callum was gone.

Ivy drew herself up and checked one more time over the wall. He wasn't there; he hadn't been there at all.

He was gone.

Through the hole in the wall.

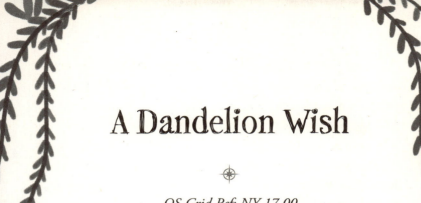

A Dandelion Wish

OS Grid Ref: NY 17 00

Ivy sat in the window seat in her bedroom, watching the hole in the wall from a safe distance. She had that prickling sensation tingling up and down her ears and neck again, and she felt like she had swallowed a pebble. Her mind moved so quickly it was hard to keep up.

Callum was a bird. A small, auburn bird with a white, speckled belly, if she was remembering it right. With feathers that flared out like fingers. She opened her *Pocket Guide to Birds of Prey* and turned straight to the page about kestrels.

She was right. Callum was a kestrel.

At that thought she felt her heart pick up speed again and her breathing turn shallow. So many questions were bubbling in her brain, and she didn't know any of the answers.

But it didn't matter how. It didn't matter why. All that mattered was that Callum had been turned into a bird and was trapped in that place.

Because what she had seen through the hole in the wall was not the same as what she could see beyond the garden wall now, from above. The world through the wall was a different place entirely.

So where was it, exactly?

No. That didn't matter either. Callum had gone into that other place, which meant it must be a place he could come back from. As a boy. Not a bird.

Ivy uncurled her fingers and stared at her palm. In the centre of it rested a round pebble, dusky pink in colour, with thready veins of black and white. She had thought it was a marble at first, but it was not quite perfect, in the way of all beautiful, natural things. It was only an odd coincidence that it was almost perfectly round.

This was what Callum had pressed into her hand in that last moment before his fingers had become… feathers.

Ivy turned her back on the world outside. She contemplated the safe nest of her tent, and the idea of curling up inside it and going to sleep. She might wake up and find that she had imagined the whole thing. The urge was so strong it was like a weight pressing down on her.

She could tell her mum. Iona would pack a bag and march out in search of her son at once, no questions asked. Ivy knew in her heart that if she explained what she had seen, her mum would believe her, even as she was struggling to believe it herself.

But if she told Iona, that would mean telling her what she had done. Or failed to do. That Callum had called for her help and she hadn't been able to go to him. That she had been too afraid, and because of it, Callum was gone.

The wave of guilt that washed over her was so strong she had to close her eyes.

She had to set this right herself.

She would have to go through the wall and find the bird that was Callum. But how could she possibly do that when she had barely strayed beyond the garden wall for the best part of a year? When she couldn't even make it to school on foot?

No. Her only clue to all of this was the stone. And if she wanted to learn about a stone, there was only one place to go. She was halfway down the stairs when there was a shout from below.

"Ivy!" Iona's voice rang up from the ground floor. "Did you find him?"

Ivy froze on the stairs, then cleared her throat and called back. "Yes!" she lied, thinking quickly. "He was in the garden after all. Filip came and invited him over for the night. I said it was fine."

"Oh good. They can feed him!"

Ivy waited until Iona's footsteps drifted away and the door to the studio creaked closed, then she ran the last few steps to Callum's bedroom.

She held up the stone to examine it again while she walked slowly around the room. Somehow it didn't look like any of the pebbles Callum had collected in jars. It was too round, the pink too vivid. Somehow it didn't quite belong.

She sank down onto the bed and sighed. Jostled by her movement, the book on Callum's pillow slid down to her hand. The green cloth-bound hardback had to be one of Iona's, borrowed from the stacks in her studio. Printed on the spine in gold lettering were the words *Folk Tales and Fairy Places of Cumbria*. On the front cover was a strange illustration, also etched in gold: a series of uneven round shapes, spaced in a wide circle.

Callum didn't normally go in for this sort of book; usually he read wrinkled choose-your-own-adventure books from decades ago or flicked through dry geological tomes just to look at the pictures. So what could he have seen in this book?

She began to turn the pages of densely printed text, which were broken up here and there by black-and-white photographs. There were pictures of familiar plants and places, but nothing particularly caught her eye – until she reached the photo of the pebbles. They were as almost-perfectly round as the stone in her hand, and even in monochrome, she could tell they were a kaleidoscope of larger-than-life colours.

Certain stones found in becks in the north
of England are known as 'fairy beads'.
They belong to the fey folk and are imbued
with magic charms which are bestowed on
the one who holds them, such as spells for
protection, courage and good luck.

Ivy looked again at the penny-sized pebble she held
in her hand. If it was a magic stone that she held, surely
she would feel something – a humming, buzzing, the
enchantment emanating out of it. It just felt like a stone.

Then again – why had Callum wanted so desperately
to give it to her?

If this *was* a fairy bead, maybe that meant that other
place – through the wall – was the fairies' world…

Fairies. Was she seriously considering this? Fairies at
the bottom of the garden?

But she had seen what had happened to Callum, and
there was no way to explain that – except magic. If she
had seen Callum transform… then anything was possible.

But how would Callum have known how to get into
a fairy world?

Ivy flicked to the index at the back of the book
and scanned its columns. There was nothing for
ENTRANCE, nothing for *DOOR*… But there was an
interesting word: *PASSAGES*. She turned to the page.

It wasn't much. A grainy photo of the rocky base of a
cliff, with a caption that read:

At the foot of Castle Crag lie two great
boulders which are said to constitute a
passage between our world and the fairy
realm beneath. Portals to this realm are easily
accessed by the fey folk, but to humans
they appear only when needed. People
who have passed through have reported
believing they had been gone for a single
day, only to discover that a hundred years
had passed in their own world by the time
they returned home again.

Ivy quickly skimmed the rest of the page, but there
was no more mention of passages or other worlds.

Callum paid attention to stones in a way no one else
she knew – maybe no one else in the world – did. So
perhaps he had noticed the hole in the drystone wall
and decided to explore.

Or maybe it had appeared to him because he had
been looking for a way in.

She peered out of Callum's window at the garden wall.
The sun was only just beginning to set, but it was setting.
In the morning her mum would realise that Callum was
gone, and how was Ivy going to explain where?

Her heart felt like it was beating in her throat. Could
there really be fairies? Could there really be another
world through the hole in the wall?

She flicked to the next page just in case there was
anything more about ways into the fairy world, but

no such luck. The page showed only a picture of a dandelion, with the caption:

It is a well-known tradition to blow on the seeds from a dandelion seedhead and make a wish as they drift away. What many people don't realise, however, is that this is a common method of communication used by the fairies. Messages have even been passed between our realms in this way.

Ivy felt a blossom of hope in her chest. There were dandelions gone to seed all over the garden. If she explained the situation and asked for help, maybe some kind soul in the fairy realm (*if there really is a fairy realm,* she added sensibly to herself) would bring Callum back to her.

With a sudden wild hope, Ivy hopped off the window seat and headed outside. Now the house cast a long shadow over the garden, and the grass was cold underfoot. It took only a moment to find a long, stemmy dandelion with a spherical silver head.

She approached the hole in the wall, avoiding looking directly at it as she knelt down on the grass and cradled the dandelion head in her palm. She wasn't sure exactly how this system was supposed to work.

"Um… My name is Ivy North," she whispered into her cupped hand. "My little brother, Callum, has been turned into a kestrel. I'm not sure how or by who, but he seems to be stuck in your world, and… well we really need him back, that's all." She paused, considering her next words. "If you're listening to this message, if you can help, please… just bring him home."

It didn't seem like enough. She had nothing to offer in return. But she had to try… What else could she do?

Ivy angled the dandelion in front of the hole in the wall, took a deep breath, and blew. Every last seed detached from the stem and floated through between the stones, a silver cloud that shimmered like a shoal of fish. Ivy's gaze followed them, and then she found herself risking a glance at the world on the other side.

The outline of the fells looked the same, that was true. The hillside in front of her sloped away at the same angle; she could hear the beck running at the foot of the valley.

But the grass was a darker shade of green, as though the sun didn't quite reach it, and there were no shadows. When she finally talked herself into looking up, she found that she could see no sun at all, no pink streaks of cloud criss-crossing the sky. What she saw was like a painting of a sky, weirdly static, a bruised purple colour.

She looked away, scrambling to her feet.

No. That was not her world.

That was not her world at all.

The Way In

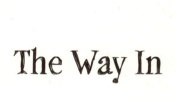

OS Grid Ref: NY 17 00

Ivy barely slept. She kept creeping back to the window, keeping a watchful vigil over the hole in the wall just in case there was any activity. But beneath the uncertainty of waiting, guilt and dread turned her organs to stone. If the dandelion message didn't work, there was only one thing for it. Somehow, she would have to go through herself.

She woke to find herself slumped on the window seat with her cheek pressed against the glass. The sky was alight with the pink glow of dawn, and two floors below she could hear her mum already at work. She tiptoed down the stairs and out the front door, leaving a dark trail of footsteps in the dew-tipped grass as she made her way towards the wall. What if there was a reply? What if there wasn't? Which would be worse?

She was just reminding herself that it was completely mad to think that there were fairies at all, let alone in another world at the bottom of her garden, when she realised there was *something there*.

Ivy ran the last few steps and crouched down, hardly daring to touch it at first. It was a seashell, no bigger than her thumb, blue and white like old ceramics, curling to a point. She reached out and picked it up. There was no burst of sparks or fireworks, no booming voice, no words written with a sparkler. None of the magic she had wondered if she might see. There wasn't even a note scribbled on the outside.

Was this her reply?

She sat with her back against the wall beside the hole, turning the shell over and over in her fingers. It had to be there for a reason. It had to be there for her.

The salty texture of the shell against the soft skin of her hands brought back a sudden memory of the last time she had sat on St Bees beach, more than a year ago, with Iona at her side and Callum playing in the rock pools. Iona had told Ivy to hold the shell up to her ear – that she would hear the ocean roaring inside it.

Ivy lifted the shell to her ear now, holding it close, and heard the beating of waves.

And then there was a voice.

"*Ivy*," a woman whispered. "*Only you can find your brother. Come through the wall. Seek out Long Meg.*"

Ivy's mouth fell open, her fingers tingling. She stared at the shell in her palm for a moment, then raised it to her ear again.

There was nothing but the hoarse thrumming of the ocean.

✦

When Ivy stepped back into the house, the door closed with a loud click. She flinched; all she wanted was to get back up the stairs to her room and start making a plan. Fairies were real and she was going to have to go into their world to find Callum; the last thing she needed was—

"Is that you, Ivy?" Iona called from the studio.

"Yes, Mum." Ivy tried to sound as busy as possible as she crept past the door.

"Couldn't bring me a cup of tea, could you?"

While the kettle boiled Ivy tried to organise her thoughts, but it wasn't easy to do so in the clutter of their kitchen. Despite Iona's best efforts to maintain a semblance of order for Callum's sake, the debris of their daily life bubbled over. The wooden surfaces were strewn with unopened letters and lengths of ribbon, assorted seedlings, half-burned candles, and jars filled with corks and sea glass and elastic bands.

It would have to be her. The message in the shell had made Ivy's heart plummet, but there was a tiny part of her – tucked away, deep down, in her middle toe or behind her ears somewhere – that felt a spark of excitement. For the first time in a long time, she was making plans for an adventure. She had no choice. It was both terrifying and wonderful.

Most importantly, she would need her map of Cumbria. That other place had seemed similar to the world she knew, so the map and a compass would be essential. Plenty of water, rations, matches, the tent, her sleeping bag and mat, a waterproof coat, her boots of course, and the fairy bead… She had better bring that, because it was tied into this whole mess one way or another.

"You're a million miles away this morning," Iona said when Ivy set the cup of tea on the table beside her mum, who was manipulating a red hunk of clay into a tall, slender vase. "I know it's cheesy, but you just have to take one step at a time. One step beyond the garden wall, and then another, and another."

Ivy felt the tightness in her chest ease ever so slightly. "It is cheesy." She smiled. "But thanks. I think I'll spend the day outside, see how far I can get."

She slipped out of the room before Iona had a chance to mention Callum. It was time to prepare in earnest.

Ivy filled a tub with cashews and raisins and blocks of chocolate, like she always used to do before a hike. She cut a generous chunk of cheddar and folded it up in a beeswax wrap, then sliced through half the warm loaf of bread her mum had baked that morning and tucked it away in a cloth bag with a drawstring. There were a few dehydrated meals in the cupboards from past adventures, quite possibly years out of date, but she pinched those too.

She had no idea whether she'd be able to find anything to eat on the other side, or indeed whether she ought to eat it if she did. She only had enough room for a couple of days' worth of food and water, and it might take her weeks to find Callum…

How long could he survive as a bird? Could he eat? How well could he fly? What if those finches were still chasing him?

Back in her room, her perpetual preparedness finally proved its worth. All she had to do was pack up the tent, sleeping bag and mat and fit them into her rucksack, which was already stuffed with everything she might need for a camping trip in the fells.

Her phone was switched off in her bedside table, and she toyed with the idea of taking it with her, but there was never any signal round here anyway, and somehow she doubted she'd find any in a fairy realm.

Ivy wound her auburn hair in a long plait and changed into her best hiking trousers and an old T-shirt. She tucked the fairy bead into her pocket. The weight of it was reassuring, because whether or not it was magic, it felt like a connection to Callum. He had given it to her for a reason. She slipped the now-quiet seashell in beside it.

Heaving the heavy rucksack onto her back, she picked up her map from the window seat and ran a finger along one of the long cracks in the cover, then tucked it into a side pocket of the pack. She was as ready as she was going to be.

She tiptoed downstairs. The pottery wheel's drone was drowned out by pop music blasting on the radio and Iona's off-key singing.

Her mum! She would have to leave a note.

Ivy slipped back into the kitchen and tore a scrap off

an old electricity bill to scribble on. She left the note tucked into the handle of the kettle, the only place Iona was bound to find it.

Mum,

Gone to get Callum. He's not at Filip's. Sorry I lied, but I know where he is and I'll get him back.
Tell you all about it when we get home.
Please don't worry.

Ivy x

It seemed extremely unlikely that Iona would read this note and not worry, but who knew — maybe they'd even be back before she made her next cup of tea.

The sight of her hiking boots made Ivy's stomach drop. Still caked with dried mud from their last excursion, they were stiff when she pulled them on, but her feet slipped into their old grooves easily. She was lucky that they still fit. When she stood up and felt the weight of them, she felt at once grounded and strong.

Ivy stepped out of the front door and set off down the garden.

There was no going back now. She knew that if she let anything turn her back towards the house, she would lose her nerve completely.

She heard a huff of breath and the sound of paws

thudding on the grass, and Grendel went speeding past her. He stopped to sniff at the hole in the wall, tail wagging as he looked back at Ivy.

"You're coming too?" she asked affectionately as she gave him a scratch behind the ears. Ivy crouched down by the wall, placing one hand as an anchor on the sun-warmed stone. She took a moment to breathe and steady herself, then peered through.

The world beyond was quiet and still, a twilit landscape. There was nothing obviously threatening about it, except its strangeness.

She risked a glance at the sky. It was pale and purple and not the sky she knew at all.

She pulled out the map and studied it. The contours of the land in front of her seemed to match those charted on the map. Even so, it had been the best part of a year since she'd walked more than a few hundred metres from her house without incident. How could she set out there with no route, no paths memorised?

One step beyond the garden wall, and then another, and another.

Callum was in there somewhere.

Ivy folded the map back with Beckfoot at its centre. She touched her fingertips to the pink stone in her pocket.

Grendel was watching her, tail wagging and tongue lolling, and when she looked his way he straightened out his front legs and dropped down in an obvious invitation to play. Then, in a flash of black-and-white like a swooping magpie, he leapt through the hole into the other world.

Ivy blinked after him. There was nothing for it now.

She placed her hands on the wall at either side of the hole. The way was clear before her. Adrenaline rushed through her limbs, filling her bones with air, like a bird's.

Her fingers drummed on the old stones. It was now or never.

Ivy took a deep breath, and pulled herself through the hole in the wall.

The Sleeping Wood

OS Grid Ref: SD 17 99

The air was suddenly filled with more birdsong than Ivy had ever heard in one place before – the evensong of blackbirds, the cooing of wood pigeons, the chatter of sparrows and the warble of blackcaps. The trees trembled with the weight of the birds jumping and dancing in their branches.

Their leaves were a spectrum of colour, muted by the strange light, but they seemed to have chosen their own season and gone with it, heedless to the weather. Some bare trunks blossomed with pink and white flowers; others were in full, vibrant green leaf; still others were crowned in autumnal gold and bronze. Some had thrown the seasons out of the window all together and bore leaves of astral blue and starlight silver.

As Ivy gazed around, rooted to the spot, Grendel galloped back and forth across the grass, stopping here and there to press his nose to the ground and drink in the smells. There were Herdwick and Swaledale sheep on the hills with colourful splotches daubed on their wool, just like the smit marks that the farmers around Beckfoot used to distinguish between their flocks – but instead of reds and blues, these were splashed with iridescent gold and silver, shimmering purple and midnight black.

Slowly, Ivy lifted her eyes from the hills to the sky above, and a quick scan confirmed that there really was no sun there. There was only that pale purple glow and the strange stillness, like looking up at the bioluminescent roof of a great cavern far, far above.

Was it even a sky at all?

She took her map out of its pocket and held it firmly in both hands, confirming her position again. The layers of the fells stretched out before her in darkening hues of violet. She risked a glance down at her feet, planted on the grass in this familiar but alien place. She didn't even know where to go, let alone how to find the path that would lead her there.

The grey fog hung around the edges of her vision like a curtain waiting to close.

There were so many birds around, but if Callum – in kestrel form – were nearby, he'd be soaring above them all. She tried to bring to mind the call of a kestrel, but she couldn't form the sound in her head. She was certain she'd recognise it when she heard it, even amongst the clamour.

He didn't seem to be here waiting for her. She had seen those birds drive him off. She'd have to do as the shell had suggested.

Only you can find your brother. Come through the wall. Seek out Long Meg.

But who *was* Long Meg? There was something familiar about the name.

Looking down into the valley she could see the beck and the woodland on its bank, but though she squinted at it, Ivy couldn't quite see the footpath that she knew passed along the far side in her world. She scrutinised the map to make sure the path was marked – yes. It should be there; she'd just have to go down and investigate more closely.

Slowly, she started to walk. She kept the trees in the centre of her line of sight and moved towards them, trying not to worry about what was or was not beneath her feet. The slope lent her momentum until she was trotting down to the beck, Grendel at her side. At the foot of the hill they leapt the small stream. Ivy's boots thudded with satisfaction onto the opposite bank.

She looked back the way she had come, a smile jumping to her lips, and then stilled. In the branches of an alder tree she had just passed beneath, a row of three birds sat motionless. They weren't singing or moving busily about like the others; they were just staring at her. Their feathers were auburn, wheaten and earthy brown, their eyes ringed in black.

Ivy cleared her throat, but still they didn't move. She backed away until the trees closed around her, obscuring the birds from view. Then she turned away.

She just needed to find a path she knew; then she could work out what to do next.

Ivy and Grendel were quickly swallowed up by the

woodland. The trees here all seemed to be in agreement that it was early summer; there was a luscious green canopy above and a carpet of moss and pungent wild garlic at their feet. The multitude of leaves overhead rustled against each other like a breeze was sweeping through them, though the air felt still. *Sssssssssh*, they whispered. *Sssssssssh*.

It was quieter in here than it had been on the hillside. The birds were still singing, but it was a subdued song that one flock of birds seemed to pass to the next, a kind of lullaby that flooded Ivy with calm and tranquillity.

Normally he raced ahead, but Grendel's steps were becoming slower, his head drooping slightly. Ivy didn't mind; her limbs were feeling very heavy, too. Her sleepless night seemed to be catching up with her, and the moss underfoot looked temptingly soft.

When Ivy looked dozily into the branches overhead, she noticed a small bird following their progress, hopping from tree limb to tree limb. It was another of those autumnal-coloured finches, and wasn't there something strange about that? She couldn't seem to get her mind to focus…

Ivy tripped hard, suddenly, the weight of her pack bowling her over. After a grunt of pain she pulled herself quickly to her feet: nothing but grazed palms. She looked back at the obstacle she had fallen over. It was a stone – a very odd stone. In fact, as she inspected it more closely, she realised it was the shape of a sleeping badger, curled up with its nose tucked into its tail.

Strange.

Ivy tried to shake the weariness from her bones and plod onwards, but Grendel had decided to lie down beside the badger-stone and she had to give him a push to get him moving. They needed to get through this wood to the path on the other side; from there she could chart a course, make a plan.

But she had to blink furiously to keep her eyelids from closing, and every trunk looked like an inviting place to lean back and rest. A grey squirrel lay curled in a tree hollow at dog-height, apparently unfussed by Grendel. As they passed Ivy looked curiously at it and realised that it was grey because – like the badger – it was made of stone.

She told herself that these were nothing more than carvings that had been placed in the wood by some kooky artist like her mum. But even Grendel seemed disturbed by the squirrel, half-moons of white in his eyes as he plodded onwards.

On they went, and there was a sparrow puffed up on a low branch, its head tucked beneath one wing. Ivy moved closer in wonder – then reeled backwards. Though its chest rose and fell as it slept, one of the sparrow's wings had turned cold and hard, and there was a greyness seeping into the rest of its body.

Ivy moved on with a distinct sense of unease. The sooner they could get out of this twilit wood, the better.

They reached a break in the trees where the violet light filtered through more brightly. In the centre of the clearing was a moss-covered boulder; Ivy remembered the place from days spent playing with Callum in her version of these woods. But even through the haze of her sleepiness, Ivy could see that there was something out of place about the scene before her.

There, huddled behind the boulder, was a boy.

Kit Kepple

OS Grid Ref: SD 17 99

The boy sat with his back against the boulder, his knees drawn up to his chest, his eyes closed. He didn't move a muscle as Ivy walked closer, and she began to wonder… had he gone the way of those other sleeping creatures? But there was still colour in his freckled white face, framed by a shock of black curls. His feet, though, in practical leather boots, looked solid and heavy, tinged with grey.

Grendel trotted over to the boy first, tail wagging like he was greeting an old friend. His tongue darted out to lick at the boy's hands and clothing, and after a moment the boy began to stir. First his head bobbed, then his eyes opened, and finally a smile lit his face as he laughed and reached out to rub the dog behind the ears. He turned to look at Ivy; his bright smile may have been intended for Grendel, but when it was turned on her Ivy felt an answering smile jump to her mouth at once.

Her body flooded with relief – another human! In this place!

Ivy walked over and sat down in front of him. "Hello. I'm Ivy North," she said. "What's your name?"

The boy sighed very deeply, as though waking from a good dream. "Christopher Kepple," he said belatedly. "But I go by Kit. Is this your dog?"

"Yes! Well, no, not really. His name's Grendel."

"He's beautiful," said Kit, who hadn't stopped stroking Grendel since he'd woken. "Out for a walk, are you? Don't you think it's strange weather today?"

Ivy found herself murmuring agreement, though it seemed like an odd thing to say. "What are you doing down here?" she asked. She wondered if it might be considered rude to ask a person how they ended up in a fairy realm, but it was hard to think clearly when her eyelids felt so heavy.

Kit ran a hand through his curly hair, screwing up his mouth. "It's a funny thing," he began. "I was looking for my older brother, but I lost him. So I tried to head back home, but – well, it's a bit embarrassing really – I got a bit lost myself. I think it's been a few days now. I really must get home soon… If I could just find Billy I'm sure he'd set me right, and we could be on our way."

"Hmm." There was something rather odd about this explanation.

"I know it's silly." His cheeks flushed pink. "It isn't like me at all. I was convinced he was just around the corner, that's why I didn't take a map or owt with me." He glanced at the map in her hands and swallowed, then a far-off gaze took over. "My parents must be really worried."

This isn't right, Ivy said to herself. This boy didn't seem to understand where they were. But how was she meant to break the news to him? She would keep questioning – just to be sure.

"I'm looking for my brother as well," she told him. "I came through the hole in the wall. How did you get here?"

"What wall?" Kit made a funny purse-lipped face as he attempted to stop a yawn without covering his mouth.

"The drystone wall around my garden, just south-east of Beckfoot," she said. "Through the woods and up the hill there. Where do you live?"

"Mardale Green," he answered. "Not far from Shap."

"I've never heard of it," Ivy said, which certainly seemed strange, because she had almost memorised her map.

"Well, it's only a small village." He shrugged. "I can't say I know Beckfoot well."

Ivy hesitated. It took a moment to collect her thoughts; really, she needed to lie down and have a quick nap. "I have to say," she began carefully, "I don't think we're in Cumbria at all."

Kit frowned at her. "Could we have crossed into Yorkshire? I don't think I could have wandered that far."

"We're not in Yorkshire," Ivy said.

Kit looked blearily around the trees, his eyes clouded with confusion.

Ivy felt like everything was taking on the haze of the

first waking moments of the morning. She had come through the wall, and walked to the wood. There had been the badger… the sleeping badger, who had turned to stone. And the squirrel, and the sparrow…

Her thoughts sharpened, just for a moment. She looked down at Kit's boots.

"I think we should stand up." She got to her feet abruptly, tugging at Kit's arm. He straightened up with her, but when she took a step away, he just seemed to sway.

"My feet are heavy," he said dumbly.

Ivy's heart fluttered. "Try to take a step."

With great effort, he managed to lift one foot off the ground and set it down again. Then the other. "What's going on?" he said with a tremor of panic.

"How long have you been sleeping for?" she asked him.

His eyes flickered as he racked his brain, but then he shook his head. "I don't know."

"I think we need to leave the woods." Ivy nudged Grendel awake; he had fallen asleep between clumps of daffodils. She took Kit's arm and held on tightly as he took one laboured step after another, and gradually his movements became lighter.

The moment they stepped out of the trees, Ivy felt the tiredness lifting, like a morning mist burned away by the sun. When Kit turned to her, the glazed look in his eyes was gone. He wiggled his feet; his boots were entirely tan now, not a hint of grey.

"I was dreaming about a wood," he said, looking back with trepidation at the wall of trees looming over them.

"It wasn't a dream," Ivy said. "This is real. But it isn't Cumbria. Not *our* Cumbria."

Kit pressed his fingers to his temples and rubbed as though to clear a headache. "But I followed Billy," he said. "I followed him around the corner, but he was gone. And I didn't know where I was."

"I came in here after my brother as well," said Ivy. "His name's Callum. I couldn't find him yesterday, so I went out looking. When I found him… he was through the garden wall. Not on the other side of it, but *through* it, in another place. Then something happened, and… he was turned into a bird. By magic. And he flew away."

She cleared her throat, aware of how she sounded. But there was no other way to explain it. "So today I came through after him, and that's where we are now – *through* the hole in the wall. This isn't our world," she concluded, "although it looks very similar. I think we're in a fairy realm."

A small crease appeared between Kit's brows as he turned over what she'd said. "It is an odd time of year not to bump into ramblers," he admitted. "I thought it might be this strange weather…" He looked up at the not-sky again and his face fell. "Gosh," he mumbled.

"What happened with Billy?" Ivy asked. "You followed him here, but what were you doing in the fells in the first place?"

"That's the funny thing," Kit answered. "I hadn't seen

him in a long, long time, and then – there he was."

Ivy waited. Kit took a deep breath. "It was Sunday, because I had the afternoon off. I decided to go up to the crags to do a bit of climbing. Billy was the one who got me into it. We used to go up and climb together, but after he went away, I started bouldering by myself. I'm pretty good at it now."

"Where did he go?" Ivy asked.

"Joined the army," Kit answered shortly; his shoulders tensed. "Went away to fight. We barely saw him for three years. He came home on leave occasionally, but less and less as it went on. Anyway, that day it was gloriously sunny. I was at Castle Crag, halfway up a tricky problem and got stuck. And then there's Billy on the ground! I couldn't believe it. He talked me through it, helped me get to the top of the crag. He was so pleased. I'd never finished that climb before."

Kit paused. "He said, 'Meet me at the pub. I'll buy you a beer.' He was laughing and I knew he was joking, but then he really did walk off. I shouted after him to wait for me and ran down, the long way round down the slope. He'd gone around the northern side of the crag for some reason, which isn't really the way home, and he'd walked between these two big boulders. I went after, calling for him, but I couldn't see him anywhere. I squeezed in between the boulders, and – well, I was surprised I hadn't noticed how late it had become. It suddenly seemed to be dusk.

"I couldn't find Billy anywhere. I remember searching

the fells around our valley, but it got dark and I got lost. After that... I remember walking. Just walking and walking, for days on end, it felt like. I lost track of time, of where I was, sometimes I even forgot what I was looking for. I remember feeling afraid, confused, lonely. But there isn't much I remember clearly before I got to this wood. Slipping in and out of sleep... it made everything that came before it feel like a dream. And then... you came along."

His gaze settled on Ivy; to her surprise, he was grinning. "I can't tell you how good it is to see another person."

She took the measure of him then. She was one of the tallest in her class, but he matched her height easily. About her age, she thought. He was plainly dressed: old boots, worn brown trousers, a white shirt with a sleeveless woollen jumper. The overall impression reminded her a bit of her granddad.

Grendel hadn't stopped trying to lick Kit's hands since they'd left the woods; well, not until Kit had let him jump up and place his front paws on his belly. The collie was now panting in contentment while Kit stroked his head absently. It had to be said that Grendel was an excellent judge of character.

Ivy considered the obvious possibility before them. When she had tried to picture her quest, she had always been by herself. She had never imagined encountering another lost human soul down here, but she already felt so much less alone.

"Since we're both in search of missing brothers, maybe we should look for them together?" she ventured.

Kit swallowed, his Adam's apple seeming to hover for a moment around a response. "So you're telling me your brother's a bird?" he clarified.

Ivy nodded once. "A kestrel."

He looked at her directly, his gaze assessing. "You seem trustworthy." There was a smile in his voice. "I'll believe you. Even though it sounds like nonsense."

"Twenty-four hours ago I would have said the same thing," Ivy laughed.

He drummed his fingers against his thigh. Then he extended his hand. "Of course. I'd be happy to have your company."

She shook his hand; the skin was tough, as though he spent a lot of time outdoors. She tried to disguise the flush of relief that crept into her cheeks by moving on with the plan.

"Okay then… We have two missing brothers, at least one definitely a bird. You don't know where to start, but I have a clue. It's why I came through. I had a message that told me to look for someone called Long Meg, but I have no idea who she is or where to find her."

"Long Meg?" Kit repeated. "Where have I heard that name before?" He crouched down to Grendel's level to rub the dog's cheeks. "I've never met anyone called Long Meg – it's an odd name for a person. Matter of fact… it's a place, isn't it? Long Meg. I'm sure it's a place!"

Ivy blinked stupidly at him for a moment, then a

switch flicked in her head. She took out her map and spread it out between them on the ground. "Of course! I've seen it before…"

Kit joined her in leaning over the unfolded chart of the county and they scanned it together for a few quiet moments. At Ivy's sharp intake of breath, Kit looked up.

"Here!" Her finger found the spot and tapped it. '*Long Meg and Her Daughters*' was written in italics over the symbol of what appeared to be… "A rock?"

"It's a stone circle!" Kit exclaimed. "I remember now. Long Meg and Her Daughters. My great-granddad had a farm near there where my dad used to spend his summers as a lad. The stones have been there for thousands of years – and the biggest one is called Long Meg."

"Long Meg is a stone?" Ivy repeated, her excitement ebbing away. "But… how are we supposed to ask a stone for help?"

Wayfinding

OS Grid Ref: NY 36 14

There seemed to be nothing for it but to start walking. Long Meg wasn't close by: forty miles as the crow flies, and they weren't crows. It had been mid-morning when Ivy passed through the wall, but without the sun in the sky it was impossible to say what time of day it was now.

"Do you know the time?" she asked Kit, who was wearing an unusual watch. He held it out for her to inspect: it had a brass cover, like a pocket watch, but when she popped it open she found the hands unmoving.

"It hasn't been working," Kit began. "Not for…" But as he cast his mind back, words seemed to escape him. Ivy released the watch and it hung loosely from his wrist; it must be a hand-me-down.

"That's all right." An uneasy memory tickled the back of her mind. Something the book had said about time passing differently in the fairy realm. Who knew how long Callum had spent here before she had seen him through the wall?

"Is your pack full of supplies?" Kit asked with a trace of wonder.

Ivy shifted the heavy bag self-consciously. "Well, yeah."

He reached out his arms. "Let me carry some. I can't let you be the packhorse."

"It's fine, honestly," she said, but after a moment's contemplation she handed him one of her water bottles. "Okay, take this. We might have to make it last. I don't know if we can drink the water here."

Kit looked at the metallic cylinder curiously, but didn't say anything.

"When did you last eat?" Ivy asked.

Kit looked sheepish again, and that was all the answer she needed. She hauled the pack off her shoulders and dug out the trail mix. He accepted a few blocks of chocolate with obvious glee.

They plotted a rough course, as direct as possible, from Beckfoot across to Little Salkeld, where they would find Long Meg and somehow ask for her help. The journey would take them a couple of days at least, even at a fast clip. Ivy chewed the inside of her cheek with frustration; two days felt unbearably slow. Every moment that passed, Callum was out there alone.

She lifted her pack back onto her shoulders and held up the map. The relief of escaping the sleeping wood had been enough to distract her from the lack of a path beneath her feet, but she was already feeling dread creep back into her bones. The strange, still sky was heavy overhead.

She needed a path underfoot, and soon.

According to the route they'd plotted, the footpath they needed should be running right past them. But when Ivy glanced from the map to the ground, all she saw was grass.

"Is something wrong?" Kit asked. He stood ready to follow her, but she hadn't even taken a step yet.

"Look." Ivy tilted the map towards him. "It should be here. Everything so far has been identical to Cumbria, but the path isn't here." She tried to swallow the distress in her voice before he noticed it.

Kit folded his arms as he considered. "Maybe we aren't where we think we are?"

"No." Ivy shook her head firmly. "I know this place. I've been here so many times in our world! I know there's a footpath here."

Her heart was beginning to beat more heavily, her breath quickening. She scrutinised the map more closely, following her route from the garden wall, down the hillside, through the wood…

If the footpaths weren't where they were supposed to be, she didn't have a hope. It was too much; she felt her vision start to swim with grey, her eyes betraying her.

Kit tapped her shoulder. "Ivy. Look."

She lowered the map.

Beneath their feet, the ground was beginning to tremble and shift. The grass was growing in reverse, shrinking back into the earth. Stones were being pushed up from beneath. The path rolled out in front of them like a red carpet, except it was only the beaten brown earth of a well-used footpath.

"What…?" It was the only word she could grasp.

Kit was laughing, an infectious, hiccupping laugh. But Ivy was too overcome with relief to join him.

"You summoned the path for us," said Kit.

Ivy couldn't speak. Yet the grey was receding, the world clarifying before her eyes. The paths *were* there; she just had to find them.

Kit set off at once, leading the way. Ivy hurried to catch up to him, and every scuff of her boots on the trail brought a growing sense of groundedness into her body.

"So this hasn't happened to you before?" she asked.

He plucked a stem of cow parsley from the side of the path, twirling it in his fingers. "No," he said. "But I never knew where I was going. Not after the first little while, when I was looking for Billy near home… Maybe that's the difference – knowing where you need to go."

The cow parsley had stilled and she sensed that he was thinking about his time alone, before she had found him. The idea of being lost in this place terrified her.

"Hopefully Long Meg will have some answers," she said, trying to sound reassuring. At this point, it was their only hope.

Kit proved himself to be a fast walker, which tended to put people pretty high in Ivy's estimation. He did have a habit of whistling tunelessly as he trudged along, but Grendel seemed to like it, and whatever made Grendel happy was all right by Ivy. He trotted along between them, tail wagging, for all the world as if he was safe at home instead of in a mysterious fairy realm.

Ivy wished she could share Grendel's ease. She avoided looking at the sky out of habit. The birds continued to sing over each other, and sheep *baa*ed on the hillside, but dread still weighed her down.

Every so often Ivy would stop, consult her map, check the surrounding fells, check the curve of the path ahead of them and the landmarks behind them, compare what she saw to what was depicted on the map, and take a bearing.

But when she stopped for what might have been the dozenth time and began to go through her ritual, she realised that Kit was watching her, rolling a long stem of grass between his teeth.

"Are you all right?" he asked, sounding genuinely concerned.

"I just have to be sure of where we are." Ivy tilted the map so that it blocked him from her field of vision and she didn't have to meet his eyes. She wished he hadn't already noticed; she wished she wasn't so obvious. But she had to check.

Then she checked again, because what she found just didn't seem right.

"We're coming through Langdale Valley, aren't we?" Kit said, noticing her double take. "I've been keeping an

eye on the fells since you found us on the map. But…"
She heard the certainty fade from his voice. "I must have
let my mind wander."

"That's the thing." Ivy lowered the map. "That fell
ahead of us is Helvellyn."

The grass fell from Kit's mouth. "It can't be," he said,
perplexed.

"It should have taken us a day at least to get this
far," said Ivy. "But it feels like it's only been a couple of
hours."

And yet, there was no doubting where they were.

As the implications of this sunk in, Ivy began to feel
some of the tension ease out of her muscles. If they were
moving this fast, they'd be at Long Meg in no time!

She consulted the map one last time to confirm their
location. If she was right, then they were currently
standing in the approximate location of the main road
north to Keswick.

No sooner had she thought this than the ground began
to quake beneath their feet again. They backed away
from the trembling soil and watched in astonishment as
a tarmac road unfurled itself, leading from one horizon
to the other, winding out of sight.

Ivy's breath caught in astonishment.

Kit walked out onto the tarmac, prodding it with his
boots as though testing the feel of it. He glanced back
at Ivy. "What is this?" he asked.

"Sorry," Ivy apologised at once. "I was thinking
about the road to Keswick. But this means you're right!

It seems like when you know about a path, it appears. I'll try not to think of roads in future. Might cause a bit of disturbance."

She giggled, but somehow Kit didn't look reassured. He closed his mouth, which had been hanging open, then crossed to the far side. "I don't know this part of Cumbria as well as I thought," he muttered. Ivy wasn't sure if she was meant to have heard him.

For a time, it felt as though they might have been the only people in the world. They saw what looked like a shepherd on a far hillside, surrounded by sheep, and there was smoke rising from the chimneys of farmhouses in the valleys.

The air was strangely still and mild. Not a whisper of a breeze rustled the grass, nor were there clouds to cast cool shadows or sprinkle rain upon them. There was no heat from an absent sun, nor was there a chill in the air. It was almost the scariest thing about the place. Back home, you were either being buffeted by strong winds, drenched in a persistent drizzle, or unexpectedly sunburnt on a surprising warm day.

"Has it rained at all since you've been here?" Ivy asked Kit out of the blue.

"No!" he replied, sounding relieved to have someone to discuss it with. "It's been so weird. Not a breath of wind either."

No sooner had these words left his mouth than a sudden gust washed over them both and a shadow passed overhead. The sound of wingbeats engulfed them, and Ivy craned her neck back, blinking against the rising dust.

There was a person flying over their heads.

Obviously, it was no ordinary person. They were dressed like an ordinary person, that was true. They were shaped very much like a person. But the main point of difference was the wings.

They were not insect wings, like in the old *Flower Fairies* books Ivy had on her bookshelf. These were birds' wings, strong and feathered and big. In this case, they looked very much like a magpie's, solid black with long fingers of white spread out in flight.

To Ivy's shock, Kit started jumping up and down beside her, waving his arms over his head. "Hey! Down here!"

Immediately Ivy grabbed his arms and pulled them down. "What are you doing?!" she said hoarsely. "We don't know if they're friendly!"

Kit rolled his eyes. "Fairies are always friendly, aren't they? Don't worry! We can ask about Long Meg. After all, we haven't actually figured out *how* we're going to talk to a stone, have we? And they might've seen Billy."

To Ivy's horror, she realised that the fairy had come swooping back towards them, winging low over the hillside until she touched down lightly on her feet, tucking her wings in neatly behind her back.

Her skin was sun-baked and weather-beaten, and her black hair was pulled back into a messy bun. She wore a bobbled woollen jumper, jeans and wellies, looking for all the world as if she was just on her way out to feed the animals. The woman looked them up and down, then stared with particular surprise at their wingless backs and shoulders. She frowned.

"Oh. Humans," she sighed. "Who let you in? I've got a lot to do this morning…" She glanced at her wrist as though there was a watch there, but there clearly wasn't.

Ivy tried to process the sight of a woman with bird's wings. She found herself temporarily unable to form words, but Kit was already talking.

"Hello there! We've lost our brothers and we're supposed to talk to Long Meg, but she's a stone, so we were just wondering if you know how we might be able to speak to her?" The words came out in a rush.

The woman rolled her eyes. "You're not the first children to wander down here and get yourselves lost," she said in a weary tone. "You'll work it out." Then something caught her eye in the distance; there was another figure flying past. "That's Glen to trim the horses," she said with relief. "GLEN!" she shouted as she launched into the air, sending up another gust of wind that almost knocked them over.

Kit and Ivy stood side by side, staring after the two figures as they flew away.

"Okay. Fairies aren't friendly then," Ivy said.

Kit's cheeks flushed pink. "*That* fairy wasn't friendly," he countered, but his voice wavered.

Ivy brushed the seashell in her pocket, tucked in beside the stone, and wondered. If this was how humans were received down here, who had sent her the message of encouragement? Or had it really just been a way of saying *stop bothering us and do it yourself*?

It seemed they would have to figure this one out on their own.

The Circle of Stones

OS Grid Ref: NY 57 37

Ivy tried to put thoughts of the fairy behind her as they continued on their way. Whenever they needed to turn onto a new path, her hands would start to tremble and her breath to quicken, but then she would consult her map and picture the route in her mind, and the path would unroll itself. Every time, she felt a surge of relief in her chest, as though it had been squeezed tight until the way lay clear before them.

Kit didn't ask to see the map, but from time to time a path popped up before Ivy had even visualised it, and she would turn to see Kit grinning beside her.

Though the landscape didn't blur as they passed, and they didn't leave a cloud of dust behind them like in the cartoons, somehow they were travelling much faster than they should have been. Before they knew it, they were on the banks of Ullswater. The long lake snaked in an S-shape away from them, the still water glowing in shades of iris that mirrored the not-sky above.

They passed along a hillside above a village. There

were figures in the streets and a few in the sky, but neither Ivy nor Kit felt quite ready for another encounter with the fairies. In fact, Ivy felt she'd be happy if they could just make it to Long Meg without encountering another soul, work things out themselves and get home as quickly as possible.

Thankfully the only living creatures that took notice of their progress were the birds. A seagull had been wheeling in slow circles overhead for a while, and Ivy was beginning to wonder if it was following them.

In an astonishingly short amount of time they passed a sign, rotting and half-covered with moss, that read:

LITTLE SALKELD ⟩

"This is where my dad's granddad had his farm. We must be nearly there," said Kit.

Ivy followed Kit across the fields until they crested a hill and saw the dark hulking shapes of great stones ahead. It was a huge circle, more than a hundred metres across, with two winter-bare, silver-barked trees at its centre that reached out with crooked limbs.

The stones ranged in colour from shades of burnt umber to dull white and blue-grey; a few even glittered faintly in the light. Some of them lay half-buried as if toppled over by the weight of years; others were narrow and stretched up taller than a person.

Kit and Ivy wandered around the circle, soaking it all in. Ivy was amazed that Iona had never brought her and Callum there before. Maybe she was saving it for a really special occasion, because there was no doubting this place would sing to Callum's soul.

When Ivy saw Long Meg, she knew her at once.

The tallest of the stones stood apart from the circle, looking down over them all. Even if Kit had climbed onto Ivy's shoulders, Long Meg still would have towered over them. She was the earthy-red hue of fresh clay, and rough to the touch.

There were impressions in her surface that looked like concentric circles, one inside the other. One near to Ivy's knees, another at the level of her waist, and another by her head. Without thinking, Ivy reached out and brushed a finger over the markings, tracing them from outside to in, one after the other.

She didn't notice Kit come up behind her, but she heard his intake of breath when the markings began to glow. Even after everything she had experienced so far that day, Ivy's breath caught in wonder at the sight of the strange light radiating from the carvings.

When nothing more happened, Ivy pressed an ear to the stone, but there was no sound from within. She scanned it from head to foot, then began to walk around it.

"Oh," she said in gentle surprise as she reached the other side. Words had appeared which had not been etched into the rock before, but now glowed the same luminescent silver as the carvings.

When rises the moon over Salkeld,
the witches are out at their work,
in their focus forgetting their limit draws close,
and midnight tolls at the kirk.

Their magic is not yet returned to the earth,
the spellwork snares round their wrists,
and roots every last witch into the ground,
transforms her to stone where she twists.

Now they sit silent until a new age
shall come and the magic release them,
but to those who settle their number correctly
Long Meg may answer one question.

Once, you may falter, but twice, on your guard,
you shall not walk away from a third.
The sisters shall welcome you into their number
if from your lips slips the wrong word.

"I'm not sure I understand..." Ivy said, scanning the words again. "Where are the witches?"

"I remember this story!" Kit's face was suddenly alight. "My nan loves this kind of thing; she's told me this one... The *stones* are the witches. They shouldn't have been practising magic after midnight, so it turned on them… It turned them to stone."

Ivy looked out at the vast circle of great unmoving rocks and felt a new eeriness settle over the place.

Kit shuddered. "*Settle their number*," he read aloud. "So we just have to count the stones correctly. But we only get three chances…"

"… or we'll be turned to stone as well," Ivy finished for him. She met his eyes with alarm.

"Are we certain that Meg can help?" Kit wondered aloud. "Just, from the story, magic doesn't exactly sound trustworthy."

Ivy let out a breath. "It's the only clue I have," she said, though the same doubt was bothering her. "But I don't expect you to risk getting turned to stone. I'll do this on my own."

At that, he just laughed. "No way," he said. "I *saw* the other animals in that wood, Ivy. The sleeping badger, the squirrel, all stone. My feet weren't just heavy because I was tired. You and Grendel saved me. So we're doing this together." When he grinned like that, with the wrinkles in his nose, Ivy couldn't help but smile back.

She looked out at the stones. "We'll call Meg number one."

They set off around the circle together, their feet rustling through the overgrown grass, Grendel bounding alongside them. They paced the circle's circumference, and each time they passed a stone they both called out the number. Some, long since fallen and half-buried in the overgrown grass, were nearly missed. It was a long walk around, and when they returned to their starting point they confirmed the number between them.

Ivy glanced up at Long Meg. She couldn't see the writing from this side, but the spirals still shone silver. "Fifty-nine!" she called to the sentinel stone.

For a moment, nothing happened at all. Then the markings glowed a deep amber, flickering like starlight, and finally turned back to silver.

Ivy felt like her heart had dropped into her stomach. "We were wrong." It was a blow – but she should have known it wouldn't be so straightforward.

"I'm sure we were right!" Kit protested. He drummed his fingers on the stone closest to them, looking out across the circle. "What if we walk separately, one of us on the inside of the circle, one on the outside? Then we can't miss any."

Ivy couldn't think of a better plan, so off they went. Ivy counted each stone from the outside, Kit from the inside. When they returned to Long Meg for a second time, Kit exclaimed, "It's sixty-two! We missed three last time."

"NO!" Ivy shouted over him, but it was too late; the colour of the markings was already shifting from silver to amber.

"I got a different number! We have to check with each other before we yell it out!" she groaned. But Kit looked so contrite with his hand slapped over his mouth and his eyes wide that her frustration just drained away.

She took a deep breath and rubbed her face with her hands. "This is our last try," she said, and was surprised to hear her voice come out in a squeak. "We *have* to get it right."

Kit lowered his hand, but his lips were pursed in thought. "One of us walks on the inside, one on the outside. One person counts, and the other repeats their number back to them. Then we can let each other know if we notice owt different."

Ivy wasn't sure it was enough, but she couldn't think of what more they could possibly do. Getting turned into stone was one thing, and yes, the idea terrified her, but abandoning Callum here – that thought was a thousand times worse.

She stationed herself on the inside of the circle and walked along with Kit as he made his way around the perimeter. He called out a number and she called it back to him, one after another, until they were halfway around.

"Twenty-eight," he called out.

Ivy jumped and shouted, "Stop!"

Kit paused. "What is it?"

"Did you say twenty-eight already?"

"Yes…"

"But there's nothing there!"

Kit looked around him. "I'm counting this stone right here." He pointed at the space between them, where there was no stone at all. She shook her head.

"What?" He came over to her, skirting around the

70

edge of the stone that was not there, and looked back at where he had been standing. His eyebrows shot up. "Where did it go?"

"Start again!" Ivy said. "I'll walk with you. On the inside. We each place a hand on every stone."

Kit took his orders without argument. They strode back across the circle to Long Meg, and each placed a hand on her sandpapery shoulders.

"One," they said together, and began to walk.

As they made their way around, one of them would occasionally reach out for a stone and find that their hand passed straight through it. Once, Ivy's knee bumped against a stone she could not see at all, and she brought Kit's hand over to it so that they could both count it. From then on they moved very carefully.

They moved especially slowly between the final stones, shuffling their feet through the long grass to ensure nothing hidden or invisible was missed. They reached out in unison for the last stone.

"What do you have?" Ivy asked, and Kit whispered the number in her ear. "I have the same. But we've got to be sure."

Around they went again, using every trick they had learned until finally they arrived before Long Meg once again. Ivy mouthed the number to Kit, and he nodded.

She turned to face the monolith and gulped. If they were wrong, she would be standing in this spot for a very, very long time. It would be much safer just to walk away.

But this was Callum.

"Sixty-six!" she called.

For a moment, nothing happened; then the markings grew steadily brighter, and suddenly faded away completely.

Ivy felt her chest tighten. She gazed hopefully around the circle. Would all the witches wake? Would they dance and hug one another, and get back to the work they had been at, however many years ago?

Or were she and Kit about to find themselves entombed in stone for a thousand years?

She heard the soft rustling of rabbits moving through the grass, undisturbed by a watchful Grendel, and the quick spring song of robins. Then a deep sigh resonated, and a powerful, gravelly voice reached them.

"Come here, children."

When Kit and Ivy turned their heads to the voice's source, they saw the face of Long Meg for the first time. The stone itself hadn't moved, but the monolith had taken the shape of a very tall woman, hunched over as though confined in a tight space. She was still the colour and texture of sandstone, and though her limbs and features shifted slightly, the stone itself remained still: like a carving in motion.

The two of them approached reverently. Even Grendel slunk around Kit's ankles and kept his head low.

"One question each," said Long Meg when they stopped before her. Every word seemed to come at great effort, but there was the curve of a smile on her lips.

Kit nodded encouragingly to Ivy. Though the stone witch's eyes were kind, Ivy found herself struggling to hold her sharp gaze.

"It's about my brother," she said at last. "He was turned into a bird, and I'm trying to find him. I don't know why or who might have done it, but I haven't seen him since I got here. Do you... do you know where he is?"

The stone woman took a deep breath, her chest rising and falling slowly within the confines of the stone. "Describe... what you saw."

Ivy tried quickly to gather the important threads of the story. "He was running towards me, and I heard this chanting sort of singing, and his arms turned into wings..." She remembered how he had reached out to her, how feathers had grown from his palms. She dropped her eyes, and her fingers closed around the smooth stone in her pocket.

"Hmmmmm," said Long Meg, drawing the sound out. "Singing, indeed... A spellwork. There's only one fairy whose spellworks take the form of songs. His name is Taliesin... once bard to a great king. I suggest you start... by talking to him."

"Where can I find him?" Ivy asked at once, hope blooming in her chest.

Long Meg only looked at her. "One question," she repeated, not impatiently.

Ivy felt like she could burst with all the questions she wanted to ask, but she held her tongue because it was

Kit's turn to speak, and he had risked being turned to stone for her.

Taliesin. Who was Taliesin? And what had Callum done to offend him?

Kit stepped forward, hands tucked deep into the pockets of his trousers. "I'm looking for my brother, too. His name's Billy. William Kepple. Have you seen him?" The naked hope in his voice made Ivy's chest ache.

Long Meg was quiet for a moment, her heavy-lidded eyes closing and opening again slowly. "I remember… a boy who looked like you. But he isn't here in Underfell any more… He just passed through."

Kit, who had brightened for a brief moment, deflated once more. "What do you mean? That can't be right!" he protested.

Long Meg shook her head within her sandstone frame. "That is all I can tell you. Now I must return to my sleep… Farewell, children."

"Wait!" Kit called desperately, but Long Meg seemed not to hear him.

She let out a deep breath, her eyes falling closed, and in the next moment there was no trace of her eyelids at all, nor of her face, nor her stooped body. Long Meg was no more than a stone again.

Taliesin, Ivy thought, the name resounding in her mind.

Beside her, Kit stood numbly with his arms hanging at his sides.

"What does she mean, *he just passed through*?"

Langwathby Tup Fair

OS Grid Ref: NY 57 34

To Ivy's surprise the violet light was beginning to darken to shades of purple, so they agreed to make camp for the night while they considered Long Meg's words. They set up in the centre of the circle, as though the ring of witches might protect them.

As Ivy pulled out the parts of her tent and began assembling it, Kit looked on curiously.

"Gosh. Your tent looks like the real deal," he said. "You should see mine! The canvas is so heavy. It kills me, carrying it around. I wish I'd had a chance to bring proper supplies."

Ivy chucked her sleeping bag at him. "You can use this," she said. "That or the tent. It's only one-person, so it's snug."

Kit gave the sleeping bag an approving once-over. "I'll be happy under the stars."

The real meaning of his words occurred to them at the same time, and they looked up in unison. Ivy squinted at the sky at first, afraid of the panic that was bound to follow her curiosity, but it was so different from anything she was used to back home that her fear was overtaken by wonder. There *were* stars, of a sort. Pinpricks of unmoving white light glowed brightly above as the not-sky grew dark. The steady spray of lights reminded her of glowing crystals in the roof of a cave.

She lay with the tent door unzipped, watching as Kit rolled out the sleeping bag nearby. The birds were finally starting to fall quiet, though the silence that replaced their song was less comforting. In the branches of the two great trees at the heart of the circle, Ivy saw a pair of those same, strange finches that had chased Callum shifting and chattering quietly together.

"Kit, do you know what those birds are?" Ivy asked.

He peered at them for a second and then said, "Hawfinches, aren't they?"

"Hawfinches?" Ivy repeated with awe. "Really? They're so rare – I've never seen one before!"

"Rare?" Kit repeated. "That's interesting. They're fairly common where I'm from."

"Is that right?" Ivy said with surprise. She really needed to visit this Mardale Green. She couldn't understand why she'd never heard of it.

Kit wriggled into the sleeping bag, got comfortable, then chewed on his bottom lip for a moment. "Have you heard of King Eveling? The fairy king?" His tone was too casual; he wasn't meeting her eye.

"No." Ivy wished she hadn't left that fairy book sitting on her window seat, or at least had had the good sense to read it cover to cover before she'd left. But there hadn't been time.

"Eveling is the fairy king of Cumbria," Kit explained, gazing up into the branches of the trees. "According to Nan's stories, anyway. She said he lived with his court at Ravenglass, and if you could find him, he would grant you a wish in exchange for a gift. I never paid it any mind, because fairies aren't real, except – well they are, aren't they, so maybe King Eveling is too."

"I don't know that story," Ivy said.

"If we go to him and give him something, maybe he'll be able to take us straight to Billy and Callum." Kit's eyes sparkled with hope.

"Maybe…" Ivy saw his face flicker at the uncertainty in her voice. "I just – Long Meg said that I should find Taliesin, so that seems like the most logical thing to do next."

Kit's face was set. "We don't know that everything Long Meg said was true," he said steadily.

"No," Ivy said cautiously, afraid she was upsetting him. He had been so good to her until now, coming all this way and risking himself. But still… she wanted desperately to continue on the path laid ahead of her. "What if," she began, thinking quickly, "what if we find Taliesin and speak to him, and if we can reason with him about Callum, maybe he'll be able to help us find Billy too? And if nothing comes of that, we'll go to Eveling next. I promise."

Grendel came trotting over at that moment and settled in beside Kit with a contented sigh. This seemed to soften Kit's mood. "All right," he said, rubbing Grendel's belly. "But how are we going to find Taliesin?"

Ivy had been pondering this herself. "I think we might need to consult some more fairies." Her voice betrayed how little she wanted to do that. "We could try walking into the village at Little Salkeld. There must be someone there. We don't know that they're all awful."

Kit huffed a laugh and lay down. "I thought it was *me* convincing *you* of that."

"I know." Ivy settled back into her tent, resting her head on her folded jumper. Then she thought back to the stone witch's words. "Did you notice what Long Meg called this place? She said its name was Underfell."

"She did, didn't she?" Kit remarked, but he sounded distracted, and she realised he must be recalling everything Meg had said.

"What she said about your brother—" Ivy began.

"*He just passed through,*" Kit cut her off. "Well, I don't know what that's supposed to mean. He has to be here. Maybe she just meant he's not in this area any more."

"I'm happy to keep looking together," Ivy said. "As long as you are."

It was quiet for a long moment. "I have to find him, Ivy," Kit said. "I have to."

When she stirred in the violet half-light and recognised the tent around her, for a blissful moment Ivy thought that she had fallen asleep in her bedroom. Then the truth hit her – she was in Underfell. She was in a fairy realm, and Callum was lost, and their mum had no idea where they were. For a few sinking seconds, panic threatened to overwhelm her.

She grabbed the map from beneath her makeshift pillow and pulled it out. *There*. Her finger tapped the stone symbol and the words *Long Meg and Her Daughters*.

You're right there, she said to herself. *Just not exactly.*

She reached into her pocket for the rose-coloured fairy bead and rolled it between her fingers, waiting to feel something – any indication that there was more to this stone than met the eye. A little electric shock, maybe, or a glow…

It was the only link she had to Callum, and as far as magical links go, it could have been better. It could have given her the power to see through his eyes – that would have been helpful. Or allowed them to communicate. Was this the reason that Callum had come to Underfell? Why had he wanted her to have it? What could possibly have made it worth being transformed into a bird?

She felt tension building in her chest. Even though she had a clue – Taliesin – she still hadn't the faintest idea where her brother was. He could be anywhere in this shifting sea of fells and lakes, and here she was lost in the middle of it.

A greyish tinge started creeping in around the edges of her vision. Ivy closed her eyes to push it away, shoved the fairy bead back into her pocket and unzipped the door of the tent.

The air was humming with insects, and birds flitted round happily, snatching them out of the sky. Rabbits were hopping through the long grass around the stones, and a fox slipped away between the trees at the far end of the field. Ivy felt her worry evaporate.

Kit was gone, the sleeping bag in a crumpled heap, and Grendel was nowhere in sight. She crept out to the hedge to pee and by the time she came back, Kit was returning from the other side of the hill with Grendel at his side. He carried both of their water bottles, freshly refilled from the nearby beck.

"I think it's this or go thirsty," he said with a wry smile as he handed hers over, dripping. "Let me know if I turn into an otter." He took a few long gulps and glanced down at himself. Ivy gave him a thumbs up and had a sip of her own.

The three of them shared a couple of slices of bread and cheese for breakfast, then broke camp.

Ivy waved at Long Meg as they set off down the hillside, but the stone gave no reply. They were following the same track that had led them into the stone circle, but out in the other direction towards the village, which would be tucked at the foot of the hill.

But when they came around the bend that ought to have revealed it, there was nothing there. Only empty pasture bordered by trees. Ivy stopped, pulled out her map, and checked again. Yes – the village should be there.

"Underfell isn't playing by the rules," Kit said with a tut. But he looked unnerved.

Ivy was trying to calm a flutter of anxiety by staring even harder at the map. "It should be here," she said aloud. "We know it should be here."

She stared at the grassy meadow, willing the buildings to spring out of the ground like the paths they'd been following. The ground didn't even tremble.

She realised she was clutching the map so tightly it was beginning to crumple under her fingers, and loosened her grip. It was all right. There was still a path under her feet.

"We'll just go somewhere else." She forced steadiness into her voice.

"Back to the other village we passed," Kit supplied. "There were fairies there we could ask about Taliesin."

"Yes." She was grateful for his calmness, and especially for not commenting on her reaction. When she lowered the map he beckoned her onwards with a wave of his arm.

But when they passed through the gate at the far end of the meadow-where-the-village-should-be, Ivy was startled to discover a freshly painted wooden sign staked into the grass verge beside the path.

TODAY!
LANGWATHBY
TUP FAIR
SPECTATORS WELCOME

"What's a tup?" Ivy asked.

Kit immediately hiccuped with laughter. "A ram, Ivy! Don't tell me you don't know that! A Cumbrian who doesn't know about sheep? Don't your parents farm?"

Ivy shook her head. "My mum's a ceramicist. She makes pottery."

Kit frowned. "What, like bowls and cups?"

"Yes. And decorative things, vases and stuff."

Kit's eyebrows shot up, but he didn't seem to have anything further to say.

"We should go," Ivy suggested. "There'll have to be someone we can ask there."

The sign pointed down the hill in the other direction, and Ivy could see that further along there was another sign, and then another, leading off around the trees. When Ivy consulted her map, she realised that the village would be just beyond the woodland in the valley.

They made their way down to it through the trees, and as they grew closer Ivy began to hear a crackling, resonant humming noise. After a day of nothing but birdsong and running water, the sound was so alien that at first Ivy tried to identify what kind of animal could be making such a sound. Finally she realised it was a voice over a tannoy giving an indecipherable commentary.

When they emerged from the trees the tup fair was right before them: marquees with signs hanging over their entrances, rings marked out with ropes, temporary fencing around yards filled with sheep. Kit stared at it all in wonder like he'd just discovered an amusement park. People were flooding in from the surrounding village and the fields beyond.

No, not people – fairies.

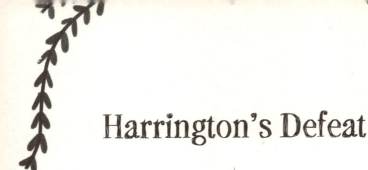

Harrington's Defeat

OS Grid Ref: NY 57 34

Just like the first fairy they had met, the fairies at the tup fair looked almost exactly like humans. They wore clothes that seemed to be from many different time periods: corsets and ripped jeans, saris and top hats, shoulder pads and bonnets, and one person in a heavy chainmail shirt and board shorts. It was as though they had access to a wardrobe from all of history and had been able to choose whatever they wanted.

There was also the matter of their wings.

There was a small boy with the wings of a wren, speckled with white and striped with dark russet shades, flung out wide as he ran after a loose goat. A willowy woman bore wings of long, iridescent blue-grey feathers: a heron. A stout person with jet-black hair and raven's wings led a tup along at the end of a rope. They were all talking excitedly in some of the thickest Cumbrian accents Ivy had ever heard.

At the sight of the sheep Grendel began wagging his tail furiously, but Ivy told him to heel and he stayed close by as they entered the showgrounds. A trembling, ruddy-faced old man with worn seagull's wings was making his slow way over to the marquee marked **HOME INDUSTRIES**, where a display of cakes was being laid out, but Kit intercepted him.

"Hello there, sir – I'm looking for someone and I wonder if—"

"Here, carry this!" The old man thrust what he was holding into Kit's hands – a Victoria sponge on a plate, filled with butter icing and strawberry jam. "How you humans get down here I'll never know. This way, come on now." He pressed both shaking hands to his cane and led the way.

Kit dutifully carried the cake to the marquee, where he set it down on the display. Ivy followed, trying not to laugh.

"Now, if I could just ask you—" Kit began, but the old man spoke over him again.

"No fairy gives information away for free! That's the first thing you need to know, lad."

Kit considered this for a second. "Well, I've just helped you—"

"And that's the information I'm giving you! 'No fairy gives information away for free.' Go on now, get yerselves back to Rheged."

Kit came back over to Ivy, scratching his head. "That didn't really work."

"We've learned something, at least," Ivy said. "Fairies don't just give away information. So we'll have to give them something in return."

"But what can we offer? Work, maybe? They might trick us into working for ten years or something." Kit dropped his voice to a whisper, glancing warily at the fairy folk passing by.

Ivy adjusted her pack on her shoulders. "I'm not sure." She wished again that Kit's watch was working, that they had any sense of time in this place. Every hour that passed felt like a weight around her neck.

"WE ARE ONE ROUND AWAY FROM THE MAIN EVENT!" announced the voice over the tannoy.

Kit's eyes darted up at the speakers and Ivy saw him mouth what looked like "Magic."

There was no chance to ask him what he was talking about, though, because they were suddenly swept along by a crowd that was bearing down on the main ring. Ivy grabbed Kit's sleeve to keep them from being separated.

When the rush ended, they found themselves pressed right up against the ropes. The sheep being led into the ring had no horns, so Ivy guessed this wasn't yet the 'main event'. She half-watched as the sheep were arranged around the ring and the judging began, very aware of all the wings rustling in the crowd around them.

Suddenly Kit nudged her in the side and nodded towards the action. As Ivy watched, the judge finished making notes on his clipboard, shaking his head slightly. The face of the farmer holding the sheep in front of him fell in dismay.

But the moment the judge's back was turned, the sheep's handler chucked something at his back. It was small and green and leafy, and it clung to the man's tweed jacket, right between his robin's wings.

"That looks like stickyweed!" Ivy exclaimed. "What is he doing throwing weeds at the judge?"

The judge stopped, as though he had felt the plant landing on his clothes, but he didn't reach for it – just flipped his pencil over to rub out the notes he had made and scribble something else in their place.

"They're cheating," said Ivy under her breath as realisation dawned. "They're enchanting him!"

"Poor sportsmanship, that is." Kit kept his voice low.

The judge finished making his rounds, and the sheep belonging to the farmer who had thrown the stickyweed was declared the winner. His enchanted plant was still stuck to the judge's jacket.

The farmers and their sheep filed out of the ring and the judge made his way over to a table at the edge. He went to scratch the back of his neck and his hand brushed the stickyweed, which he flicked to the ground with a grumble.

Ivy was struck by a bolt of inspiration. "I've got an idea!" she whispered to Kit. "Follow my lead."

She ducked under the rope and trotted across the grass to the table. As she approached, she saw a box filled with purple rosettes with gold lettering that read 'JUDGE'.

"Aha! There they are." She reached in and pulled two out. She handed one to Kit, who fastened it to his jumper as though he knew exactly what they were doing.

"Excuse me?" The judge turned around just as Ivy finished affixing her own rosette.

A silver badge fastened to his tweed jacket read:

Naveen
Head Judge

"We're so glad to finally meet you, Naveen!" She held out her hand. He shook it unenthusiastically, and again she noticed that telltale glance to her shoulder blades.

"We've heard all about you," Ivy went on. "My name is Ivy and this is Kit. We've been learning to judge since we were very small. We're some of the best in the world above, but we just knew we needed to learn from you."

"Is that right?" The man looked distinctly suspicious as he withdrew his hand and adjusted his glasses. "Judges from Rheged? How did you hear about me?"

"Oh, word gets around. Legends, really," Kit said effortlessly. Ivy wanted to hug him; she could see the judge's chest puffing up at the compliment.

"This is a prestigious event to be cutting your teeth on." He looked impressed. "Very well, then. Clipboards and pencils are on the table there."

Ivy left her backpack beneath the table, guarded by Grendel. She grabbed hold of Kit's arm and whispered in his ear, "If we stop them cheating, he'll have to help us."

Kit tapped his nose, smiling widely.

Farmers had begun to enter the ring one by one with their tups. The sheep were broad and sturdy, with wool the colour of a cloudy day and curling horns at either side of their guileless white faces. Ivy was surprised to realise that a few of their handlers were as wingless as she was. Had these humans once been lost too, she wondered, or had they made their way here on purpose?

Naveen approached the first sheep. Ivy watched curiously as he felt along the ram's back, lifted its feet, and peeled back its lips to peer at its teeth. He nodded approvingly and jotted down some notes. Kit was nodding as well, and Ivy pretended to write something down.

At the next candidate, Naveen looked back over his shoulder and said to them both, "Would you like to check the teeth?"

"Absolutely!" Ivy said with forced brightness. As she stepped forwards, it occurred to her that she really should have let Kit volunteer, since he actually knew about sheep. Well, there was nothing for it now. She knelt down beside the animal, put one finger on its top lip and pushed it up so that the barest flash of white was revealed.

"Just wonderful!" She jumped back up at once. "Top marks."

Naveen looked quizzically at her. She could feel Kit's shoulders shaking with laughter beside her.

As they made their way around the semi-circle it began to seem like the competitors would be good sportspeople after all, because Ivy still hadn't seen anything suspicious. Kit seemed to have lulled Naveen back into trusting them with comments like "good-quality wool" and "looks a bit hunched".

Next they came to a woman with sandy skin and silver hair so long it reached her waist. Her wings were a merlin's, silky and grey, and her nose wrinkled when she looked at Ivy and Kit, as though there was a bad smell in the air.

"Hello, Birch," Naveen greeted her, and the fairy squeezed his shoulder familiarly. Ivy narrowed her eyes, searching for some sign that the fairy was casting a spell over the judge, but she noticed nothing.

Naveen was making approving noises and Ivy glanced over his shoulder at his marking sheet. He had scribbled *10* in every column. They had to have missed something – he was enchanted already!

And then she saw it – tucked into the collar of his shirt was a vivid green bell-shaped leaf.

A downy birch leaf.

Ivy crept up beside Naveen and brushed the leaf off his neck. It fluttered gently down to the grass.

Naveen flinched. He glared at Ivy, his mouth trying and failing to form words.

"Sorry," Ivy said, a little too loudly. "I'm just not sure I agree with your marks for the, uh, condition…"

She watched with relief as he read over what he had written, harrumphed, and flipped his pencil over to rub out the scores.

"Good work," Kit whispered to Ivy. She grinned, but the smile practically fell off her face when she saw Birch staring daggers at her.

She looked past the fairy to the next competitor – a human woman with peachy skin, pink cheeks and a grey bob. Even though Ivy had no idea what Naveen was looking for, she could tell the head judge was impressed with the woman's tup.

As they approached the final farmer – another fairy – Kit whispered in Ivy's ear, "Did you see that?"

"What?" she hissed back.

"This farmer just put a jar of gold paint back in his pocket. He was touching up the smit mark!"

"Afternoon, Mr Blackthorn." Naveen shook the man's hand. "This must be Harrington?" He reached for the sheep's haunches to assess the muscle there.

"I'll do that!" Kit cried, elbowing Naveen out of the way so he could reach the sheep first. He felt enthusiastically around the animal's back end, then stepped back. There seemed to be stars in his eyes as he grinned at them all.

"Wonderful condition!" Kit said giddily. "Never seen a tup like him!"

Naveen was shaking with silent rage. He brushed Kit aside, had a token feel along the sheep's spine, nodded and jotted something down.

Kit returned to Ivy's side, his hands covered in gold paint. He beamed at her dreamily.

Naveen walked out to the centre of the ring and

adjusted his glasses as he read over his notes and totted up scores. Kit and Ivy fidgeted behind him. There was utter silence around the ring as everyone awaited his verdict.

"This year's winner is…" Naveen said slowly, dragging out the tension, "George, owned by Mrs Heelis!"

The grey-haired human woman smiled broadly and punched the air. Ivy burst into applause.

"WHAT!" Kit cried, his face aghast. He dropped to his knees beside the gold-painted tup. "It should have been Harrington! HARRINGTON WAS ROBBED!"

The crowd burst into laughter as Ivy grabbed Kit's hands and pulled them to the ground, wiping the paint off on the grass. But no sooner had the befuddled rage faded from Kit's face than Naveen came storming over to them.

"Have you been interfering with the competition?" he asked, outraged.

Ivy straightened up, pulling Kit with her. "That's right," she said. "We did you a good deed and stopped the cheating. And now we need to ask for your help in return."

Naveen spluttered with indignation. "You shan't get anything from me! Cheating is a time-honoured tradition at the Langwathby Tup Fair!"

"Oh," said Kit.

"I'm beginning to think that you might not be judges at all!" Naveen scoffed.

A deathly hush had fallen over the watching crowd. But when Ivy glanced around, red-faced, she realised that no one was looking at the three of them at all.

There was a man standing in the centre of the ring. He had a head of long, tangled hair, with a crown nestled amongst it that looked ancient and roughly hewn. It might have been gold, but she couldn't tell because the entire figure was drained of colour, like a sketch in shades of grey. There was a haziness to his edges, the quality of a flickering screen.

He had no wings, and he was not dressed like a king, in long robes with a fur lining; instead he wore a loose, untucked shirt and plain trousers. He turned slowly towards them. The man's face was young, but his brow was furrowed. Ivy felt the moment his gaze locked on hers.

There was movement in the grass around his feet – a puddle, gradually seeping away from him in every direction…

It wasn't liquid. It wasn't *anything*.

It was colour leaching away.

He took a lumbering step, leaving behind a patch of grass bleached white and grey. There were gasps from the crowd.

"An echo!"

"The king?"

"Who has it?!"

But their voices faded away when the king took another step, brushing past one of the sheep. The farmer holding it was trembling violently, and when his prize tup began to change, he released him and staggered

93

backwards. Colourlessness bled from the tup's wool where the king's leg had brushed it, spreading over the confused creature until he was as ashen as a charcoal sketch.

All at once it was chaos. The tups bucked and strained themselves free of their handlers. The crowd scattered, shouting, swarming in all directions. Gates were left open. Fences were knocked down. Sheep frantically sought each other and ran for cover.

Ivy was rooted to the spot. A seagull shrieked overhead. She could not say when Kit had left her side or where he had gone.

The king lurched across the ring, and as he pushed past fairies and sheep in the tumult they were washed of every hue. He was coming straight towards the judges' table, and beside Ivy Naveen was standing paralysed, clutching his clipboard.

Without a moment's hesitation Ivy stepped in front, putting herself between the king and the judge. The spectre stretched out one long-fingered hand and Ivy threw her arms up in front of her face.

She felt the strength and weight of the spectre's hand even as it passed cleanly through her arm. The king hesitated and looked at his hand with a troubled crease to his brow as though it had somehow betrayed him, then he staggered backwards and fell to his knees.

He vanished before he hit the ground.

Ivy's heart was drumming so quickly in her chest it felt like it was about to explode. She fell to her knees as he had, just shy of the spot where he had disappeared. She clutched her chest as though that might help to slow her racing heart.

Kit was pushing his way through the crowd towards her, and he reached out, then hesitated. "Your arm!" he exclaimed.

Ivy peered down at the place where that cold hand had passed through. A silver handprint was seared into the pale skin of her forearm, glowing and prickling as though it had been scorched by ice.

Faster than the Helm Wind

OS Grid Ref: NY 24 19

"Yan, tyan, tethera, pethera, pip... sethera, lethera, hovera, dovera, dec..."

The wren-winged boy sat on a fencepost counting sheep in Cumbric as they came shuttling through into the pen; Grendel was busy rounding up every last loose animal.

The handprint on Ivy's arm had not faded, but by now Ivy and Kit had concluded that she was not likely to die from it any time soon. Her heart was slowly returning to its usual steady rhythm.

"He came straight for the judges' table," Kit was saying, slightly muffled by the slice of cake he had stolen from the Home Industries tent. "Why there? And why didn't he take the colour out of you, like he did everyone else?"

Ivy thought back to the moment when the Spectre King's eyes had landed on her own. She had felt his focus and his intent. He was coming for *her*. She knew it, but she didn't understand why. She turned over the apple Kit had stolen for her in her hands.

"It must be something to do with Callum. With whatever happened that led to... well, all of this."

An old fairy woman was doing the rounds with a pot of rainbow-streaked cream, which she was applying liberally to every person and animal who had lost their colour. A few of the tups were already restored to their former glory, the rich russet and smoky blue-grey flowing back into their wool.

Naveen appeared before them, badge askew, feathers ruffled. Ivy looked up at him in surprise.

"While I can't condone the prevention of cheating, it does seem that I am in your debt." He paused and cleared his throat. "You said you were in need of help."

"Yes!" Ivy said with relief. "We're looking for a fairy. His name is Taliesin."

Naveen blinked in shock. "Taliesin? Are you sure?"

"Yes," Ivy said again, but his reaction had thrown her. "Do you – do you know where we can find him?"

"I do. If you're sure you want to..." He wrung his hands, watching her uncertainly.

"We are," Ivy insisted – but then she wavered and added, "Why wouldn't we?"

Naveen's mouth was a thin line. "Only that Taliesin is a very powerful fairy indeed. Some would say the most powerful in Underfell. And he isn't fond of humans. Not at all."

Having seen what Taliesin had done to Callum, the

last part didn't come as a shock to Ivy. But to hear a fellow fairy talk about Taliesin in a tone that verged on fearful... *that* added distinctly to her unease.

She pulled the map from the rucksack on the ground beside her and unfolded it. "Can you show us where to find him?" she asked.

Naveen snatched the map from her hands and his eyes roved over it. "How Rheged has changed since I was last up above," he mused.

"Do you mean Cumbria?" Kit asked.

"You might call it that, but to us, it will always be Rheged." Naveen did not look up from the page. "That's the spot." He tapped the paper, and where his finger made contact there was a spark. He blew on the map as a small plume of smoke rose from it.

Ivy grabbed the map back from him in a flurry of panic. Where he had touched it, the paper had the tiniest of singe marks. "Thanks," she said, but it was hard to sound grateful when he had just scorched the most important object she owned.

"*Saltom*," Kit read from the spot he had marked.

"He's the mayor there," Naveen said. "And humans are *not* welcome." He beckoned for Ivy to hold out her arm and inspected the shimmering handprint closely. "Something's protecting you," he said, and then walked away without further explanation.

"What could it be?" Kit asked. Ivy stared at the imprint of the ghostly hand and wondered.

Kit went to help Grendel round up the stragglers

while Ivy plotted their route westwards. Saltom was beside Whitehaven, on the other side of the county, so it would mean trekking all the way to the coast. At their rate of travel, Ivy was hopeful they could get there in a day, but it still felt maddeningly slow to keep seeking Callum on foot.

One of the farmers gave them a bag of dog food as a thank you for Grendel's help, though it looked more like sugary pink cereal than dog kibble. Once he'd eaten, the three of them set off.

As they made their way, Ivy felt her confidence growing with every step. They were passing through some of her favourite valleys, beneath fells she had spent many happy days exploring with Iona and Callum. They were places she hadn't set foot in for more than a year. She felt astonished – almost overwhelmed – to be walking through them now, like the past year had never happened.

They were not exactly the same places – there was no doubt about that, as they passed through kaleidoscopic meadows where bluebells and snowdrops flowered side by side and birds of all descriptions chattered together in the seasonless trees, while fairies flapped disinterestedly by on their way to more important things. But each time she checked her map, confirmed where the next footpath or bridleway should be, and watched it unravel before them, she felt her resolution strengthen.

They passed along the shores of Derwentwater and began to make their way around Cat Bells. Though the strange absence of a breeze or the warmth of the sun made her skin prickle, the smell of wild garlic was in the air, and it was hard not to almost enjoy herself... until she remembered why she was there.

Callum was out there alone, and here she was, daydreaming.

"There has to be a faster way." She stopped in her tracks. Kit bumped into the back of her with an "Oof!"

"It is frustrating, backtracking like this," he agreed. "But I don't know what else we can do."

"You said your nan knew lots of stories," Ivy said, reaching for anything that might help. "Do you remember anything about... flying carpets, or seven-league boots?"

Kit screwed up his face. "Not really," he said, apologetic. "I mean, we *are* travelling fast. A lot faster than we would up above. Faster..." he trailed off, and then realisation broke across his face. "Faster than the Helm Wind," he murmured.

"What?" Ivy said, baffled.

"Don't you know that one?" Kit was already scanning the landscape around them, and suddenly he changed course and set off at a march – heading *up* the mountain, instead of around it. Ivy hurried after him.

"No! Where are we going?"

"To the top of Cat Bells. I don't remember many of the details of the story, but it was a long time ago, a thousand years at least. There was a king of Cumbria... he was the king of Rheged, like the fairies said!" As they toiled uphill, he had to catch his breath between sentences. "One night, he was at his castle – Nan says it was Mayburgh Henge, but I don't know, maybe Brougham instead – and he got word that there was an invasion by sea off St Bees, the other side of his kingdom. So he climbed to the top of the nearest hill, and he called his pony, Peregrine."

He grinned breathlessly at Ivy, who remained sceptical. "A pony?"

"Not just any pony," Kit corrected her. "A fell pony, born out of these hills. He used this special chant to summon her. I'll tell you when we get to the top. Peregrine carried him across the kingdom to the sea, and he was able to join his soldiers in time and hold back the invasion."

Ivy's nerves jangled as they ascended the mountain, passing one false peak after another. She may not have known the story, but she was anxious with hope that Kit was right.

Finally they reached the top, and rested against the cairn there to catch their breath. Then Kit straightened up, cast an uncertain look Ivy's way, and turned to look out over Derwentwater.

"Darker than a moonless night,
Older than the hills,
Faster than the Helm Wind –
Peregrine, I call upon you."

He let his voice carry as loud and as far as it could, and Ivy could see from the look on his face how much he was enjoying it.

Silence followed. It was peculiar enough just being on a summit without being deafened by an ear-aching wind, but the waiting was too much for Ivy.

"It's all right," she said after a moment. "We'll keep walking. It won't take that long." Her voice cracked on the last word and she swallowed.

Kit's expression was crestfallen, but he nodded.

Then, before either of them could take a step, the stillness was broken by a long, echoing whinny.

Ivy spun around just in time to see a shadow streaking through the air over the lake towards them. In what felt like the space of a moment they were enveloped in a smoky black cloud, and when it dispersed, there was a pony trotting around them.

Ivy's jaw dropped. A pony. That had flown across the sky. To the top of a mountain.

The creature's coat was black and gleaming, her thick mane and tail fanning out as she moved. She fixed them both with a black eye and then made a throaty whickering sound.

"Hello," Ivy said, awestruck.

"We need to offer her something," Kit murmured to Ivy. "I forgot that part."

Hastily Ivy dropped her pack and dug through the top pocket, where she was storing their food. She laughed when she found the apple Kit had nicked from Home Industries. "Will this do?" She extended her arm.

In answer, the pony crunched into the apple, brushing

Ivy's palm with her velvety lips. Ivy giggled and wiped the juice off her hands.

"I'm Kit, and this is Ivy," he introduced them. "And oh – Grendel. We need to get to Saltom. Will you carry a dog?"

Peregrine looked from Kit to the border collie at his feet and back again, then snorted.

"I hope that's a yes," Kit said. Peregrine turned side-on to offer them her back.

"I've never ridden a horse before," Ivy said with trepidation.

"It's easy. I'll give you a leg-up." Kit held out his hands to make a step. Ivy set her toes into his palm, placed her hands gently onto the soft hair of Peregrine's back, and Kit hoisted her up. She threw her leg over, only just managing not to fall right off the other side.

"I'll go in front, since you've got the pack. Here, take Grendel." Kit scooped up the dog and pushed him into Ivy's arms.

"Don't be a wriggle," Ivy warned Grendel, pulling his warm body against her chest. Kit placed his hands on Peregrine's withers and bounced on the spot before launching himself onto her back, only giving Ivy a small kick with his heel as he swung over.

Then they were all astride, and there was nothing for it but to move. "Hold on," Kit warned. Ivy could see the curve of a delighted smile on his face as he dug his hands into Peregrine's thick mane and braced himself. Ivy leaned into his back, pressing Grendel securely between them.

The dog was being remarkably calm – or perhaps he was too frightened to move.

Ivy tensed as Peregrine took her first step, then another, and began to trot towards the edge of the summit. "Wait a minute!" she said urgently as she realised what would come next, but it was too late – Peregrine had taken off into the air.

Ivy's heart hammered as they soared into the not-sky. All these months she had been avoiding looking *up*, and here she was, plunging headfirst into it. She closed her eyes and pressed her face into Grendel's warm fur. The smells of horse and dog were earthy and comforting. When she dared to open her eyes, what she saw below filled her with both dread and amazement.

The valleys, the hills, the rivers and lakes – all of it was so far away, reduced to its essential parts, that it was like looking down at her map. But her head pounded, and the grey fog teased at the edges of her vision – her body knew better. She squeezed her eyes shut and held on tightly to Grendel and Kit and Peregrine, willing them onwards.

From time to time Kit laughed and whooped, and she could feel him shifting to get a good look around, which helped to remind her that she was not alone.

At last Ivy felt her stomach rise and her head swim – they were beginning their descent. When she risked a glance, she recognised the familiar curve of the western coastline. The sea was a greyish kind of violet here, not unlike home. Waves rolled over the surface of the water, even without a moon to guide them. When she dared to look out as far as she could, Ivy saw that there was no horizon at all. The sea and the sky simply blurred together so that it wasn't clear where one ended and the other began.

Beneath her, green hills sloped down to the silver coastline. In the bay was a great, curling stone harbour, and a grey brick tower on the hill above it.

"What is that?" Kit asked, his voice whipped away by the speed of their movement.

"The Candlestick," Ivy called back. "It was a chimney for the mine. Did you never come here on a school trip?"

Kit tilted his head, craning his neck around to look at her. "Trip? My school's never been on a trip anywhere!"

"Oh," said Ivy, taken aback. "Sorry."

They came in to land in the long grass just beyond the Candlestick, on a cliff's edge high above the water. They braced themselves for Peregrine's hooves to hit the ground, but her landing was as smooth as if they'd landed on a feather bed. She cantered along the cliff before slowing to a trot, then eased to a stop.

Ivy slithered from her back first, her legs almost giving way as she hit the ground. Then she helped Grendel down; he looked as shaky as she felt. Finally, Kit hopped off with another whoop.

"I'm glad you enjoyed yourself," Ivy said, feeling sick with the built-up anxiety of their flight. She wanted nothing more than to curl into a ball and recover.

Peregrine snorted and began to walk away, but Ivy called, "Wait!"

She dug into the top of her pack and tore off a hunk of their bread, holding it out to the pony. "Thank you so much," she said. "Please, take this."

Peregrine didn't need telling twice. She plucked the bread delicately from Ivy's hands with her teeth and chewed it with evident satisfaction. Kit gave her a grateful scratch beneath her mane. Then she trotted off towards the edge of the cliff, leapt into the air, and was gone.

"I can't believe we got to ride *Peregrine*." Kit laughed. "No one is ever going to believe me!"

Ivy took a steadying breath. "You had that stored up here all along?" She tapped Kit's forehead with a finger. "What else have you got? Nothing about people transforming into animals, I suppose?"

Kit laughed, but then his face became serious. "Well, just Bega, but you know that one, right?"

The name jogged Ivy's memory. "Something about sailing to St Bees in a little round boat?"

"That's it. She was an Irish princess, with a fairy father and a human mother. Her father arranged a marriage for her, but she wouldn't go through with it. She fled across the Irish Sea in a coracle."

"But her dad put a spell on her!" Ivy added as the tale came back to her.

"Exactly. She was transformed into a seal, and she lived in the sea for years, so they say. By the time the spell was broken and she finally stepped ashore at St Bees, she had half-forgotten who she was. In some ways, the seal never fully left her. That's how Nan tells it, anyway."

Ivy's mind was churning as she tried to process what this story meant for Callum. "Are you saying that when humans are turned into animals, they can... forget who they are?"

Kit's eyes darted to the side as he quickly considered. "If Bega was half-fairy, it could have affected her differently, being an animal. Maybe Callum is safer."

"Or maybe he's much worse," Ivy countered.

If the story had an ounce of truth to it, Callum's personality, his memories, everything that made him *Callum* could be being scratched away, moment by moment.

Time was not on their side.

The Fairies of Saltom Pit

Before they could take another step, Ivy pulled out her map. Keeping her head above the waves of anxiety that threatened to pull her under, she laid her compass flat against the paper and took a bearing; she checked their surroundings, nodded, and tucked it all back into the pocket of her pack.

No fairy settlement was immediately obvious, but there was a familiar sandstone outcrop on the cliffside that seemed the natural place to start looking. The stone sank deep into the hill, run through with narrow passageways, beaten smooth by the sea. It was eerily still and quiet as they descended into the rocky avenues. Every surface was inscribed with names and dates that ranged across centuries: *LAR; 1645; John M; Gillian 1807*.

"This must be the place." Ivy ran her fingers over the indented letters. "There has to be a door somewhere."

"You think they live *in* the cliffs?" Kit squinted at a carved name so ancient and smooth it was practically illegible.

"Well, this is Saltom Rock. I guessed this was what Naveen was directing us to, because it also used to be called the Fairy Rock," Ivy explained. "My mum was making a plate about it for an exhibition – about a man who fell in love with a fairy here... He'd sail around the cliff every new moon and stay with her until the moon was full again. But one day he set sail a night early, and she wasn't there to light the beacon for him, so his boat was wrecked on the rocks and he drowned."

"Cheerful," Kit said. He was rolling a piece of sandstone between his thumb and forefinger; the movement reminded Ivy painfully of Callum. "Sounds about right. If this is the spot, I suppose we just need to find a way in."

Suddenly the beating of wings punctured the still air, and Ivy pressed herself flat against the stone. She held her breath as a chaffinch-winged fairy soared by overhead, but the fairy didn't come to land at the rock.

Ivy dug her toes into a crack in the stone and pulled herself up so that she could peek over the top of the passage. She could see down to the shore, where she watched the fairy alight on the pebbly beach beside a very peculiar structure.

At the water's edge was a tall, higgledy-piggledy brick building, with an opening at the top. From this gap protruded a huge mechanical wooden arm that bobbed and sawed, making an eerie mechanical sound amidst the birdsong and chatter of wildlife.

"I suppose you know what that is from your school

trip?" Kit said. Ivy couldn't tell if he was teasing or annoyed.

"They said it was an engine house," she said anyway. "For the mine. For Saltom Pit."

As they watched, the fairy let himself in through the wooden door set into the side of the building. He didn't come back. A few moments later two more fairies emerged from the door, chatting animatedly, and took off in flight. Ivy and Kit ducked down to hide again until they had passed overhead.

Ivy blinked. "Taliesin isn't the mayor of Saltom Rock at all…"

"He's the mayor of Saltom *Pit*," Kit finished for her. "Fairies… down a mine." He turned a shade paler at the prospect.

"I suppose that's our way in then," said Ivy. "But Naveen said humans aren't welcome. And somehow I don't see anyone offering to escort us down."

Kit climbed back onto the ledge, and Ivy followed suit. He was peering up and down the beach, mouth screwed up in thought. The tide was still a way out, exposing marine debris all along the shore. "I have an idea," he said.

For the next hour or so, the two of them combed the beach as the tide crept gradually in. Every time they heard the wingbeats of a fairy approaching or the swinging of the engine house door, they hid themselves among the rocks until the coast was clear. They gathered smooth branches of driftwood, long, rubbery clumps of seaweed, and even a handful of feathers from a spot on the shore where an unfortunate seagull must have met its end.

Ivy used her pocketknife to divest her tent of a couple of the long guy ropes she never used and cut them into small pieces. With a great deal of creativity and no small amount of frustration they fashioned themselves a fragile pair of wings, made from a driftwood frame and feathers of seaweed and kelp. Ivy fastened them carefully onto Kit's shoulders and tightened the makeshift straps. He did a slow spin.

Ivy sucked in her bottom lip. "It's a mine," she said finally. "It's going to be dark down there anyway."

Kit gave her a bemused look, as though that was not particularly helpful feedback. They did look like wings – for a split second. The shape was about right, but the texture, and certainly the briny smell, were a bit of a giveaway.

But it was the only plan they had. So, with Grendel trotting ahead, they made their way up the shore and opened the door to the engine house.

The interior of the building was dark and empty, lit only by the opening where the mechanical arm passed through. The grinding of machinery boomed around the shadowed brick space as the arm rocked back and forth, disappearing into a hole in the stone floor at the far end.

In the centre of the room was a steel cage, hanging over nothing but darkness. The old metal lift was connected by cables to a series of cogs and gears that didn't look very reassuring; it creaked slightly as it swayed. When Ivy peered down into the gloom of the shaft, she felt a warm breeze rushing up from below.

Kit gathered Grendel up in his arms and stepped across the void onto the lift. Ivy followed. It felt like stepping from a jetty onto a rocking boat: that same rush of adrenaline in the moment you're suspended over the water, the shift in your balance as the ground drifts beneath you.

Inside the lift there was a single panel with a large button that had been rubbed shiny from use. Ivy looked to Kit for assurance, but he only offered a half-smile in return.

She pressed the button.

The lift groaned and rattled and they descended into darkness.

Light crept up the mineshaft, illuminating their faces from below. Ivy realised that she had at some point taken hold of Kit's sleeve, and he was grasping a dangling strap of her backpack.

The light that filled the lift was electric blue. There was an earthy, underground smell lurking in the air, but overwhelming it was something sweet and rich, like a growing forest.

The lift jerked abruptly to a halt, and Ivy and Kit found themselves on the edge of a field.

They opened the creaking door and stepped out into rows upon rows of green leaves encircling crisp white florets of cauliflowers. Despite the fact that they were in a realm with no sun – despite the fact that they were *under the sea* in a realm with no sun – vegetables were growing. In fact, they were thriving.

Ivy felt a giggle bubble up in her chest, but she swallowed it. The cavern was quiet, and though it seemed to be empty, nothing would give away two humans in the fairies' midst like a giggle echoing round the place.

A path led from the lift through the centre of the field to a tunnel beyond. They passed through rows of potatoes and carrots, Brussels sprouts and snow peas, incongruous scarecrows standing sentinel in the soil. Ivy's eyes strayed to the packed earth above them, held up by a criss-crossing network of beams and posts. It was the only thing separating them from the sea.

Well, that and magic, she supposed. But it was a funny thing: the mineshaft gave her nowhere to go but forward, nowhere to get lost. The path was not only beneath her feet, it was all around her, funnelling her onwards. It was strangely comforting; her breath seemed to come more easily.

"Whose idea was it to build a mine under the sea?" Kit muttered uncomfortably, adjusting his jumper as his eyes darted up to the low roof over their heads.

Clearly he did not feel the same.

Ivy ran a critical eye over him, her supposed fairy host. In the unearthly blue half-light it was harder to tell that the wings were no more than beach litter. All they could do was hope that no one looked too closely.

No sooner had she thought this than a figure emerged from the tunnel: a farmer carrying a squealing piglet, dirt streaked across her face. Her wings had fawn-coloured feathers with a paintstroke of tree-bark brown splashed across each. They were corncrake wings, a rare bird Iona liked to paint on her pieces, no longer seen in Cumbria. Ivy tensed at once, but to her relief the farmer didn't spare them a second glance.

They entered the tunnel, which looked just like the photos Ivy had seen on her school trip of dark, forbidding mineshafts, where the air was thick with coal dust – except, that is, for the green. There was growth all around them: sunny yellow rattle springing up along the edges of the shaft like verdant roadside verges; ivy creeping up the walls and carpeting the roof over their heads. Underfoot was a carpet of buttercups, daisies, bog cotton and tufts of long grasses and reeds. Grendel ran around sniffing everything and joyfully rolling in the best smells.

As they walked down the mineshaft, caverns opened out to either side. There was a field of corn growing and, in another, rows of grapevines. Grendel raised his head, nostrils flaring, and suddenly went zooming off down one of the openings. When Ivy and Kit ran after him, they came upon a cave whose walls were lined with hexagonal cells like a giant beehive. The air was filled with buzzing as creatures flitted here and there. Ivy frowned as she realised what she was looking at: hedgehogs with what seemed like the fluffy tails of squirrels and the translucent wings of bees.

They backed out of the cavern, and Kit's leg bumped into a sign they had not noticed before:

> ## Do not disturb the Tizzie-Whizies!

Ivy and Kit looked at each other.

"Nowt surprises me any more," Kit said.

They carried on.

Eerie noises emerged from deep in the packed-earth walls, from the ground beneath their feet. The creaking of wheels, the rumble of heavy carts moving, grunts and shouts that sounded distressed.

"You hear that?" Kit murmured. Ivy nodded, disturbed by the unmoored sounds.

A repetitive, tinny clattering drowned out the other noises, and when they came to another opening in the side of the shaft, Ivy found herself staring down a close, narrowing passageway. At the end of it, human men with soot-blackened skin heaved pickaxes at the bedrock. They were speaking to each other, grumbling and sighing, but their voices were muffled like they were coming through an old radio.

Ivy's skin prickled with the strangeness of it. "Hello?"

she said, but the whole image immediately flickered and went out. They were left staring at an empty passage.

"It's like they're ghosts," Kit said. Ivy shivered.

These echoes of the shaft's history seemed to fade as the mine became more populated. They passed brightly painted front doors with letterboxes and numbers squashed into the earth walls at odd angles. Birds flitted overhead, not as numerous as in the realm above but occasionally zipping by as though on their way somewhere important.

As the three of them walked further down the tunnel they began to encounter more fairies, and each time Ivy felt her muscles tighten, ready to run. A group of kids with swallows' wings came racing towards them, but they were too caught up in their game to pay Kit and Ivy much attention, though they did pause to pat Grendel before they shot away again.

A middle-aged fairy man passed them by, puffing on a pipe as he rode on the front of a cart laden with chickens that clucked away in straw-filled crates. He had a florid face and a barn owl's speckled golden-brown wings. As they passed each other he narrowed his eyes and scrutinised Kit and Ivy.

"Have you got the paperwork to bring a human down here?" he demanded around his pipe.

"Of course," Kit squeaked.

The man took out his pipe and began to sniff. "What on earth is that smell?" He peered more closely at Kit's wings as they edged around his cart. "Is that seaweed?"

Ivy's heart leapt to her mouth. They squeezed themselves past the cart and set off sprinting.

"Hey!" the man shouted. His eyes bulged as he yelled after them, "Hey! Come back here!"

Luckily the cart full of chickens was too unwieldy for him to turn around and give chase. Grendel loped ahead with his tongue flapping from the side of his mouth. They were soon out of sight of the cart, and paused for a moment in an empty passage to catch their breath and gather themselves.

"I don't think I can handle much more of this," Kit said between breaths. "We need to get in and out as quickly as possible. Where exactly do you find a mayor?"

"The town hall," Ivy supplied.

"Is that marked on your map?" Kit said, and Ivy blinked at the bite of his sarcasm. "Joking," he added.

Ivy felt a small stab of hurt, nonetheless. "If they're anything like humans, and they are a bit, it'll be somewhere central, won't it? So we'll keep looking, and if it comes to it, we'll start asking around."

"Let's hope it doesn't come to it." Kit glanced over his shoulder at his disguise.

Fortunately, their question was answered very quickly.

The doorways on either side of the mineshaft became more densely packed together and the traffic in the tunnel heavier. They kept to the edges, with Kit's back turned to the wall wherever possible. Grendel was attracting a lot of coos and pats from passers-by, which seemed to distract attention from the two of them.

They rounded a bend in the tunnel and all at once the mineshaft opened into a great cavern. Here the electric blue light was brightest, and when Ivy looked up she saw the roof glowing with spirals of bright aquamarine bioluminescence. Fairies filled the paths between the buildings, jostling one another as they moved around. Wide-open shop doors were set into the cave walls, with hanging signs proclaiming: *THIRD-, FOURTH- AND FIFTH-HAND BOOKS FOR SALE! SALTOM'S FINEST TEAPOTS! BREN'S BEST BEEKEEPING SUPPLIES!*

All the chaos was centred around a huge sandstone building with a clocktower that reached up into the highest point of the cavern. A tall, wide staircase led up to a portico supported by pillars, and carved into the stone above the entrance were the words TOWN HALL.

"Gosh," said Ivy, for hanging from the pediment was a banner. It depicted a hazel-skinned man with long black hair in a ponytail, staring nobly into the middle distance. Beneath his portrait were the words:

TALIESIN
Elected your mayor for another century!

"That's handy," Kit remarked.

"A dog!" Ivy heard someone cry in delight. She discovered that Grendel was already engulfed in a crowd of excited fairies, and was accepting the affection piled

on him with lots of licks and a hint of nervousness in
his white-ringed eye.

She extracted him and climbed the steps of the town
hall at Kit's side. When the heavy doors closed behind
them, the noise and atmosphere of the town evaporated.
They found themselves in an echoing chamber of
marble floors and high ceilings, mostly empty, except
for a long, polished desk lining the far wall. Their steps
were loud as they crossed the room towards it.

The fairy at reception adjusted their glasses and
asked, "May I help you?"

Ivy looked pointedly at Kit; it wouldn't make much
sense if she was his spokesperson. "We're here to see
T-Taliesin," he stumbled, then cleared his throat and
continued confidently, "We have an appointment."

The receptionist peered at them over the top of their
spectacles. "Then you ought to know Taliesin takes all
his meetings in the Tea Rooms," they said impatiently.
"You should have been given this information. Who set
up the meeting?"

"Um," said Kit.

Standing just behind Kit, Ivy watched in dismay as a
seagull feather drifted free of its bindings and floated to
the floor. The receptionist's eyes widened as though this
were the height of embarrassment; then they frowned
and leaned forwards to peer at Kit's wings.

"His name was Leonardo," Ivy cut in. "Thanks for
your help!" She grabbed Kit's arm, spun him around
and dragged him back across the room before the

receptionist could get too close a look.

"Typical Leonardo," the receptionist grumbled behind them, but anything else they might have said was drowned out as Ivy and Kit opened the doors to the town and noise came rushing in.

They stopped halfway down the steps, where they could still see over the heads of the inhabitants of the bustling centre. Between the signs for artisan spade suppliers and boating equipment and repairs, Ivy laid eyes on a closed door with a stained-glass window depicting a teapot in shades of violet and yellow. The sign hanging from the wall above it read *SALTOM TEA ROOMS*, inside the outline of a steaming cup of tea.

They wove their way through the crowd quickly before anyone could waylay Grendel, and discovered that it was quite hard to squeeze past fairies without jostling their wings. When they reached the closed door, Ivy's hand hovered uncertainly over the handle for a moment.

The fairy who had done this thing to Callum was inside this room. He was capable of such powerful magic. By confronting him, she could be condemning herself to life as a pigeon.

But he was her only hope of tracking Callum down.

They entered a room filled with warm, yellow light. It was wallpapered in dark green and jam-packed with round tables, neatly arranged with vases of flowers and teapots and towers of cakes. Every table was full, and beneath the chatter, jazz music issued from a record player.

A waiter approached them at once. "Do you have a reservation?" he demanded.

"We're here to see Taliesin," Ivy said with authority.

"I'm sorry?" The waiter glanced distastefully at her wingless shoulders. He directed his gaze to Kit instead. "Does this human speak for you?" he asked, but almost the very moment he was finished speaking, his face fell. "Are you—?"

In the clear yellow light, the waiter was easily able to reach out and brush his fingers over the slimy seaweed surface of Kit's makeshift feathers. Neither Kit nor Ivy realised what was happening in time to stop him.

The waiter actually staggered back in horror. "Fake wings!" he exclaimed. "*Humans!* Sneaking into our establishment!"

Suddenly they had the attention of the whole room. The conversation dropped away, leaving no sound but the hum of the record player. The eyes of every fairy in the tea room landed on Ivy and Kit, their brows knitting in horror.

Ivy felt as though the ground had been pulled out from underneath her.

"Leave them be," said a voice from a booth in the far corner. "They're my guests."

That rich, resonant voice was unmistakable. Ivy had heard that voice echoing in the fells, singing her brother into a bird.

The man in the corner booth rose to his feet, and Ivy locked eyes with the fairy who had transformed her brother.

121

Taliesin

OS Grid Ref: NX 94 17

In Ivy's mind, Taliesin had been an evil sorcerer with a pointy hat and a glowing staff. Even when she had seen the banner hanging from the town hall, she had not really associated the image of that fresh-faced, smiling man with the person who had turned Callum from a boy into a bird.

Even now, she was stunned. His face was just as the portrait had depicted it, but his wings were striking: a stripe of grey at the top, followed by brown, then amber and white, and finally blue-black. The pattern was familiar, but she couldn't remember which bird it belonged to. He was also strangely ageless, his skin unlined and bright. He wore a sharp grey suit with his black hair tied back, and his mouth was curled in the shape of a smile.

His eyes, however, were shrewd.

Taliesin walked smoothly between the tables of stunned fairies, and when he reached the waiter's side he laid a hand on his shoulder. "These children are here at my invitation," he assured him. "Kit, now, I don't think there's any need for such subterfuge."

He flicked a finger dismissively, muttering a musical "*Ta-tata-tata*," and the wings, to Ivy's astonishment, shrank down to the size of a leaf and fluttered to the floor.

"Ivy. Grendel." Taliesin nodded to each of them. He opened a hand towards his booth. "Right this way."

They followed him across the room as conversation gradually resumed around them. Dirty looks were still thrown their way, though more than one hand snaked out to pat Grendel as he passed. Kit slid into the booth before Ivy, and Taliesin sat down opposite them. Grendel curled up by their feet, casting a wary look around the room before tucking his nose into his paws.

Taliesin was humming under his breath, and before any of them had a chance to speak, a menu came flying from the waiter's hands on the other side of the room, over the heads of the other customers, and he caught it deftly.

Their host scanned the options. "Ivy, yes, lavender I suspect… and Kit – it is Kit, isn't it, or do you prefer Christopher?"

Kit seemed momentarily stunned, then stuttered, "K— er, just Kit."

Taliesin smiled beatifically. He was humming again, no tune that Ivy was familiar with, and suddenly it was as though the volume in the room had been turned right down. When Taliesin called, "Matthias?" his voice was the only one that could be heard.

The waiter came running over at once, and the hubbub in the room returned to its previous clamour. No one at the other tables looked like they had even noticed, or maybe they were just used to it.

"We'll have a Marquise Grey for my friend Ivy, and a pot of three-ginger tea for Kit, thank you." The waiter took the menu and disappeared again with a nod.

Ivy found herself suddenly uselessly speechless.

"Long Meg said we should talk to you," Kit began, peering at Ivy sidelong.

"Yes, yes – straight to business, of course!" said Taliesin, who had also been watching Ivy expectantly. He turned his focus on Kit. "You're looking for two people, I take it?"

"Yes," said Kit. "Our brothers. Billy and Callum."

"Callum is presently in the form of a kestrel," said Taliesin, matter-of-factly.

"Because you turned him into one!" Ivy burst out.

Taliesin cocked his head and smiled. "That is true," he said. "Your brother came into Underfell and took something from me. He was on the verge of escaping, so I delayed him. I thought that if I turned him into a kestrel, he would drop the object he had stolen, but when I reached the scene, I couldn't find it anywhere."

"What was it?" Kit cut in.

Taliesin's searching gaze hovered on Ivy. "A fairy bead," he replied. "Do you know what that is?"

Ivy swallowed. "An enchanted stone," she said. "Is that right?"

At that moment, Matthias returned and deposited a silver pot of tea and a china teacup in front of each of them. He also placed a saucer of water on the floor for Grendel.

"You are correct," said Taliesin. "A particular stone, imbued with a particular spell, to have a particular effect on a particular person. Have you noticed the key word here?"

"They don't work on other people," Ivy replied. "Is that what you mean?"

"Quite right." With his elbows resting on the table, he clasped his hands together, watching her with birdlike intensity.

"So stealing one would be pointless," added Kit.

"Callum wouldn't steal," Ivy said flatly. *Not intentionally*, she thought, and felt suddenly troubled. Her thoughts strayed to the smooth, round pebble that right at that moment felt as though it was burning a hole in her pocket. Callum would never have taken it from someone – but what if he hadn't realised it belonged to anyone?

Though he wore a pleasant smile, Taliesin's eyes were hard. "Do you have it?" he asked her plainly.

The thought of relinquishing the stone made Ivy's mouth feel dry. She couldn't part with it – not when she still didn't know why Callum had given it to her, not when she still didn't know where he was or how to get him back.

"No," she said.

Taliesin sat back, scrutinising her. The smile faded from his lips.

"If he did take it from you, Callum probably knows where it is." Ivy tried to put an edge of steel in her voice. "So if you turn him back, we can ask him."

"Impossible," Taliesin said breezily, spreading his hands. "I haven't the foggiest idea where he is. Do you?"

Ivy frowned. "Can't you just use your magic to find him?"

He hesitated a moment, running his tongue over his teeth, and then said in a weary tone, "Clearly you have no understanding of how magic works in Underfell. Believe me when I say that I do not know where Callum is, nor do I have the power to turn him back into a boy."

There was a moment's silence.

"You haven't touched your tea!" Taliesin exclaimed, startling them all.

He hummed another tune, short and pleasant. The teapots in front of Kit and Ivy lifted into the air, tilted and filled their cups to the brim, then set themselves down again.

Kit reached out and lifted up his cup, but Ivy laid a hand over his, guiding the china cup back down.

"That's very rude," Taliesin said, and though nothing changed in his body language, there was a cautionary undercurrent to his words.

As Ivy lowered her hand, Taliesin's piercing gaze seemed to fixate on it. She realised that the silver handprint was shimmering on her arm for all to see, and hurriedly dropped it beneath the table.

But Taliesin's eyes were shining. "*Urien?*" he breathed.

"What?" Ivy said.

Taliesin looked up at her as though startled, and in a moment, his face had smoothed over again. "Your tea," he said.

"Every story I've ever heard agrees that you mustn't eat or drink anything the fairies give you," Ivy said evenly, though her heart was thudding.

Taliesin leaned back against the booth, rolling his eyes. "Or you'll be trapped in our realm forever, isn't that right? Why on earth would we want to trap humans here? We spend enough time trying to shoo lost souls back out as it is."

He held Ivy's gaze. She didn't move, and the teacups stood steaming and untouched on the table in front of them.

Taliesin let out a little laugh of disbelief, and for a split second Ivy thought she could see beyond the mask of intense politeness to a dangerous frustration bubbling beneath.

Then he leaned forwards, interlocking his fingers, the picture of calmness once more. "It is imperative to me that I retrieve that bead." There was a weight to the words that hadn't been there before. It was unnerving.

"Why?" Ivy asked.

He looked momentarily as though he were going to shoot down her question, but he studied her then finally answered. "Because it's mine."

127

"Can't you just make another one?" she asked.

"No," he said coldly.

Ivy felt a chill travel down her spine.

"Ivy." His voice was beginning to waver just slightly. "I must insist that you hand over the stone."

Ivy stared as he let his eyes fall closed and began to sing. Though quiet enough that no one at the neighbouring tables would have noticed, his voice was clear and strong. Ivy couldn't understand a word that passed his lips, but the melody was enchanting. *Exactly the kind of song that could trap you in the fairy world*, she thought absently.

She was so drawn into the tune that she didn't notice the pulling sensation at first, like someone was tugging on a string connected to her chest, urgently demanding that she act, she must do as he said—

But another sensation was blooming within her, like a speck of sunlight that grew bigger and brighter, expanding outwards, until the string broke and the song ended.

When she regained focus, she found that Taliesin was watching her with naked hostility. Kit, beside her, had a troubled crease to his brow, as though he had some inkling of what had just passed between them.

Strengthened by the golden warmth in her chest, Ivy said, "I don't have it."

Taliesin lowered his gaze to the table for a moment, and when he lifted his head again, it was Kit who had his attention. "It seems to me that you have been playing second fiddle here for some time, Christopher."

"Kit," he corrected, though he looked thrown by the fairy's remark.

"Kit," Taliesin conceded. "Try the tea, won't you?" He hummed – the barest note – and before Ivy could think or move, Kit had lifted the teacup and taken a sip. Ivy caught her breath.

Kit swallowed and shrugged. "Quite nice," he said amiably.

Nothing about his demeanour seemed to have changed, but he had not intended to drink his tea, Ivy was sure of that. Taliesin had compelled him. Just to show that he could? Or to make sure Kit felt the effects of the tea? Her breathing quickened.

A slow smile spread across Taliesin's face. "Have you tried going back to the source?" he asked, his tone too concerned, too helpful. "Looking for Billy in the place where it all began?"

Ivy watched Kit's eyes widen. "Home?" he said, like it was a magic word.

Taliesin nodded. "I suggest you pay a visit to Mardale Green. You may find some answers there."

Kit glanced at Ivy and she felt for a fleeting moment that he was unsure whether she would agree. The thought made her heart sink.

"I can only advise that when you are there, you keep clear of the *hermit* on Castle Crag." Taliesin enunciated the word with distaste. "An unfriendly character."

Kit gulped down the last of his tea. Taliesin looked

pointedly from Ivy's untouched cup to her face; she held his gaze. He let out a quick sigh and steepled his fingers.

"Let me make one last offer to you both. If you find yourselves in a tight spot and aren't able to think your way out of it, I will offer you my assistance, no matter the time or the place. I will expect the fairy bead in exchange. So let us hope that you remember its location before that eventuality."

"We've done just fine on our own so far," Ivy pointed out.

"Nevertheless. Should you miraculously discover it on your person, all you need to do is whistle." He let out two short, chirping whistles to demonstrate. "Now you."

Ivy was itching to leave this booth; it seemed easiest just to go along with the forced politeness. She repeated the whistles back to him.

Taliesin seemed satisfied; he waved them away. "Now, if you'll excuse me, you've rather disrupted my schedule. I really can't keep the Minister for Chimneys waiting any longer."

He gestured to a fairy woman waiting by the door of the tea rooms, anxiously gripping a clipboard.

Ivy's chest felt tight with frustrated expectations. Everything in her had been hoping upon hope that this would be the end of her journey. Perhaps if she handed over the fairy bead here and now he would take her to Callum and transform him into a boy at once. But he had said outright that he couldn't. Callum had given the bead to her for a reason, and her body rebelled against the idea of handing it over.

"Thank you for your time," she said, because it seemed like the right sort of thing to say at the end of a meeting. She rose from the table and Kit followed suit, Grendel leaping eagerly to his feet. Taliesin stood as they left, adjusting his tie, his face unreadable. When Ivy looked back over her shoulder, she saw that he was already welcoming the Minister for Chimneys to the table, his mask expertly in place.

The Unmapped Village

OS Grid Ref: NY 47 11

Word had spread. Despite their winglessness, nobody tried to stop Ivy and Kit as they made their way out of the mine. But fairies parted to make way for them; they whispered behind their hands and watched them pass. Only one child reached out to try to stroke Grendel, but their mother pulled them back.

It made for a much quieter journey.

Ivy was in turmoil. She was no closer to finding Callum than she had been when she arrived; he felt further away than ever, and time was ticking by. If the man responsible wasn't willing or able to find him and turn him back, who in the whole of Underfell could help her?

Kit kept plucking dandelions from the ground, nervously pulling off all their yellow petals, then doing the same again. Fairies narrowed their eyes at him when he did so, but he didn't seem to be aware of the heat of their stares.

Ivy watched him from the corner of her eye. For

all they knew, that cup of tea Taliesin had compelled him to drink had condemned Kit to live out his life in Underfell. She could only hope that Taliesin was right about the untruth of the old story.

As the crowd thinned out and they came closer to the end of the mineshaft, those echoed snatches of human suffering revisited them. Memories of shouts and thudding labour, and, once, the whisper of a child crying.

When the lift creaked to a stop, swinging over the empty shaft, they found that night had fallen. Within the engine house it was pitch black. They felt their way outside, where the pinpricks of light in the not-sky overhead illuminated the shore enough for them to find their way back up the cliffside.

Ivy doled out the sleeping bag and the tent and they made camp without really talking. Grendel had a bowl of pink kibble while Ivy and Kit shared the last of the bread and cheese. There was still the trail mix, but the dwindling supplies were a worry.

Ivy was so weighed down by disappointment it was hard to know what to say. She looked at Kit dusting bread flour from his fingers. She remembered how his face had lit up when Taliesin mentioned Mardale Green. It occurred to her that she had asked him very little about his life before Underfell. Had she really made much effort to help him at all? Guilt clenched around her heart like a fist.

Ivy reached into her pocket and pulled out the fairy

bead. She rolled it in her fingers, wondering if there was something she was supposed to figure out, some way it could help her contact Callum. Why had he wanted her to have it?

"What is that?" Kit was squinting at her in the darkness. She could only make out the shape of him, but clearly he could see that she was holding something.

Her heart skipped a beat. She had never told him.

"It's the fairy bead," she admitted.

His whole body went still. "You have the fairy bead?"

"I'm sorry I didn't tell you," she said in a rush. "I didn't mean to keep it from you! I didn't know Callum had taken it. I really don't think he stole it. He doesn't steal! If anything, he would have just misunderstood. But I don't think that's it. He came here for a reason and the last thing he did before he turned into a kestrel was put this bead into my hand."

"Why didn't you just give it to Taliesin?" Kit's raised voice made her flinch.

"I don't trust him!" she retorted. "Do you?"

He was shaking his head, his hands at his temples, but he didn't answer her question. "We've been travelling together for days. You should have told me! What if it could have helped us, or—"

"It doesn't do anything," Ivy cut in, a flush of shame rising to her cheeks. "I haven't been able to figure out what to do with it."

"What if I'd been able to help? Did you think about me at all? You didn't even consider my suggestion that we go to find King Eveling. And now we've been all over the place and we still haven't got any closer to Callum."

It was like a slap in the face. "We'll go to Mardale Green tomorrow," she said at once.

Kit wriggled into the sleeping bag. "Lucky me," he said flatly. "I've finally got your approval." And he rolled away from her with a huff.

She stared at his curled-up shape with anger running hotly through her veins. How could he act like she was telling him what to do? She had never stopped him from doing what he wanted! All she ever did was point out the most logical next step. And how ungrateful he was for it!

Ivy lay back in the tent. But within a few moments she felt an uncomfortable prickle around her diaphragm. Kit was angry with her. Cheerful, ever-smiling Kit felt let down by her. She chewed on her bottom lip.

She fell asleep with the flap open, just in case Kit decided he wanted to talk.

Ivy woke to the sound of rustling as Kit fought his way out of the sleeping bag outside. She sat up blearily, but then jolted as she caught sight of the silver handprint on her arm. She examined it now, turning her arm to catch the unearthly shimmer: a constant reminder of the Spectre King.

And what had it meant to Taliesin? He had recognised it, that was for sure. He had said something that sounded like *Urien*. But she had no idea what that meant. Except that, somehow, Taliesin was connected to the Spectre King.

She packed down the tent and stowed it in her backpack. When Kit returned he dropped her full water bottle beside her pack. She got to her feet, pulled the fairy bead out of her pocket, grabbed his hand and placed the stone in his palm.

"There it is." She tried to keep her voice steady. "What do you think?"

Though his mouth had been a thin line when she'd first taken his hand, his face softened now. He rolled the stone between his fingers, looking closely at it, tilting his head this way and that.

"It doesn't look like much," he agreed, then handed it back to her. "I'll have a proper look at it later. When we're in Mardale." His voice was solemn, but he smiled. It was a small peace offering, but she would take it.

"I'll keep it here." She tucked it into the side pocket of her pack. She didn't like the idea of not keeping it on her person, but it wouldn't be far away, and hopefully Kit would appreciate the gesture.

She took out the map and unfolded it, but suddenly Kit's hand was on the paper, pushing it down. He pointed inland, towards the fells on the horizon.

"Is that Wasdale over there?" he asked.

"Yeah."

He grinned. "That's Billy's favourite spot for climbing." He glanced at the map in her hands, and

136

his voice was hesitant. "I can get us home. I don't know every path like you do, but I know I can get us there. Can you just trust me?"

Though it almost physically pained her, Ivy nodded mutely and refolded the map. It troubled her that she had never heard of Mardale Green. She knew her map inside out, but she couldn't picture the place where the village was marked.

When they set off, her fingers tingled with the need to pull it out and check their position – just quickly, maybe when Kit wasn't looking – but she stopped herself. If she thought about it too much her heart started to thud in her chest and her eyes would stray down to the ground beneath them – no path, just the fells in the distance and Kit's certainty that he could find his way – and the world would take on a grey hue.

So she kept her eyes on Kit as he walked ahead of her, striding purposefully forwards, getting sidetracked here and there by an impressive old elm tree or some uncommon wildflowers he wanted to point out to her. She had the map and the fairy bead in her bag, and Kit to lead her onwards with his blithe, infectious assurance – everything would be all right.

Once they reached Wasdale, paths unrolled for Kit one after another like red carpets. His stride took on more confidence as the day wore on and he picked up the pace. What should have taken them days, crossing the county on foot, took a matter of hours in Underfell.

They threaded a trail that wove through valleys on

the banks of rivers and climbed high into ridgelines. Red deer nibbled the grass along their route, bold as anything, unafraid of Grendel. Sheep were everywhere too, *baa*ing from improbable cliffsides and trotting out of their way on the springy turf.

Ivy was becoming wary of the birds' incessant chatter. Taliesin had recognised her and Kit and Grendel at first glance; had even known their names. She was beginning to think that the birds might be listening. As they made their way she glanced now and then into the sky, though it still sent a shiver of unease through her. But she never saw the shape of a kestrel.

Ivy's mind kept replaying their conversation with Taliesin. Somehow she had confronted the fairy who had transformed Callum and come away with nothing at all. And if Kit's story was to be believed, with every second that passed Callum was becoming less boy and more bird, and she was failing him.

She had no route plan, no bearing on what to do next.

But they could find Billy, and that would be something.

Out of breath, they ascended a slope to a rocky peak that Kit said was called Four Stones Hill, and Grendel leapt up onto the cairn that marked its summit. Kit and Ivy stood beside it and looked out over the valley criss-crossed with stone walls. Two small lakes shone amidst the carpet of green, one feeding into the other through a wide river.

Kit shaded his eyes with a hand against the bright violet light and grinned as he took in the view. His mood had risen and risen as they'd drawn closer to his home village, measurable in the lightness of his step. "High and Low Water." He pointed to each of the lakes in turn.

Ivy couldn't remember ever hearing of two connected lakes called High and Low Water. There were only so many lakes in Cumbria; not to hear their names with a ring of familiarity seemed strange. She itched to dig out the map and scan it, but she had promised Kit. He had got her this far.

"And there – that's home!"

Ivy's gaze followed Kit's outstretched finger to a gathering of stone buildings at the head of the valley. She couldn't pick out much detail from the hilltop, but Kit swore he could see his house. His pace quickened as he led her down the slope and along the banks of the lakes. Their surfaces reflected the lavender hue of the not-sky above, and they were almost entirely still. But at the water's edge, ripples fanned out onto the pebbled shore.

They passed the lakes and made their way through farmland, along a lane that erupted before them between stone walls enclosing empty square fields. There were stones scattered across the track from places where the walls had collapsed, but not a sheep in sight.

Ivy noticed for the first time that the clamour of the birds had died away. Its absence made her muscles tense, and she kept her eyes peeled. Only a few discordant individuals chirped and sang from time to time as they walked. Ivy glanced up at one of the culprits. In a sudden rush, she realised why she had recognised Taliesin's wings. They were the same as these – the birds that were locally extinct up above but seemingly abundant in Underfell. The birds that had followed them everywhere they went. The birds that had plagued Callum and driven him away from the wall.

Hawfinches. Ivy felt suddenly unsteady.

"There's Castle Crag!" Kit pointed to the other end of the valley. On a far crag a round, windowless tower rose up out of the stone. "Although I've never seen that building before," he added, puzzled.

Ivy recalled Taliesin's words. "It must be where the hermit lives."

"Must be," Kit agreed. "But I wonder why he'd want to warn us away from it?"

Somehow Ivy didn't trust that Taliesin had their best interests at heart, but she didn't feel comfortable saying so within range of the hawfinches.

Looking ahead to the village she could see a few large buildings – a church, a pub – surrounded by houses, all hewn from the same grey stone. There were a couple of unsealed roads, already shaking themselves free of the earth as Kit paved the way ahead for them. All the buildings clustered around a humpback bridge over the river that fed out from the lakes. From this distance, there seemed to be no one there at all.

As they drew closer, Ivy noticed that some of the buildings' roofs had fallen in, leaving dark gaping maws.

A door was hanging from its hinges, the paint blistering. She felt something like panic stir in her chest, but when she looked at Kit he was smiling widely, closing his eyes and drinking in the familiar smells.

"It won't be the same down here as up above," she said to him. "Don't forget that."

He nodded absently, and it was clear he hadn't heard a word.

The church was the first building they passed up close. Its roof had collapsed in several places, its heavy door hung wide open, and stemmy, unchecked grass grew over the graves in the yard. Kit paused and took it in, pursing his lips.

"They just finished raising money for the new roof."

Ivy cleared her throat. "It's not the same place," she reminded him. "This is Mardale-Green-in-Underfell. But Billy could still be here, even if it doesn't look the way you remember it."

When he seemed unable to answer, she went on, "Where's your house?"

It was as if the words awoke him. He glanced over his shoulder at Ivy with a sudden smile so genuine that she couldn't help but smile back. "Follow me," he said.

As they made their way through the village, they were startled occasionally by the rumble of a stone tumbling from a wall or the clatter of a potted plant falling over on a doorstep. When a slate slid off a cottage roof, Grendel let out a sudden stream of barks that made them both jump.

Ivy slipped on a flat stone inlaid in the road, which

was covered with something green and slimy. Now that she looked, she could see there was a thin coating of the stuff over much of the village – garden walls, chimneys, benches. She ran a finger over the wet surface and pinched it between her fingers. Up close it looked hairy.

"It's algae," she said to Kit, but he didn't hear her.

"Here's the lonning!" he shouted happily, breaking into a run down a grassy lane overhung by yew trees. Ivy flicked away the slime and set off after him.

By the time she caught up, Kit was letting himself through a kissing gate into a garden. Ivy stepped through behind him, noticing as she did so that the gate was weighted closed with a heavy stone on a chain. Callum loved gates like this. The thought made her vision waver.

They walked up the garden path together. Kit's house looked almost intact compared to some of the others, and welcoming, with creeping ivy winding around the doorway and a neat roof of grey slate. But as they drew closer, Ivy could see that the whitewash was chipped and greening, and the windows were missing their glass.

Stepping through the unlocked front door, Kit called out, "Hello?"

His greeting echoed back to him. They went from room to room but found nothing. The house was bare: no carpets, no wallpaper, no furniture. There was a broken vase on the floor, a fork on a windowsill. Just the relics of a life left behind.

This, above and beyond everything else they had

encountered in Mardale Green so far, seemed to disturb Kit. His face was white as mist by the time they returned to the front hallway, but he didn't meet Ivy's eyes as he brushed past her and went out into the garden.

"Billy?" he called as he walked around the exterior of the house. The hedges looked like they hadn't been trimmed in decades, creating patches of eerie purple-black gloom around the garden.

Ivy followed at a distance as Kit called for his brother. She called his name herself a few times, half-hearted and quiet. The strangeness of it all made her whole body feel light.

As she stared vacantly out at the fells, they seemed to come suddenly into focus. The shape of the ridgelines was familiar, though she felt she had seen it from a slightly different angle, higher up perhaps. From… a canoe?

She stopped where she was while Kit stuck his head into the rotting garden shed and poked around. She reached over to the side pocket of her rucksack and pulled out the map. With one finger she traced the route they had followed from Saltom: the valleys, the ridgelines, Four Stones Hill. She found their location and went still.

"What are you doing?" came Kit's voice.

If he had sounded angry the night before, it was nothing compared to this. When she looked up, his face was twisted in betrayal. The sight made her chest clench.

"I told you I knew the way! We're here, aren't we?" he went on, half-furious, half-pleading. "I thought you were going to trust me!"

143

"I do trust you, I just – I don't trust Taliesin! I don't think he sent us here to find Billy. I..." Ivy trailed off, unsure how to begin to explain what the map had told her. She didn't know how. She simply held the map up before him and pointed to where they were.

"Haweswater?" Kit read out loud, the confusion clear in his voice. "What's...?"

Ivy watched his eyes dart around the map, taking in the surrounding fells. "Where are High and Low Water?" he muttered. "You're saying we're in the middle of a lake that doesn't exist. That's where the village is."

Ivy brought the map back to her chest, holding it tightly. "Haweswater is a reservoir," she said slowly. "The valley was flooded in the 1930s."

"What?" Kit's forehead creased. He shook his head. "You're having a laugh. The 1930s?"

The gears in Ivy's mind clicked: Kit's clothes, the way he had frowned at her brand of toothpaste and tent, the rare birds that were common where he came from... Her voice was urgent as she asked, "What year was it? When you saw your brother at the crag?"

Kit seemed confused by the question, but he answered her anyway. "1917."

He must have seen Ivy's eyes go wide, because there was a tremor of panic in his voice when he spoke again. "Why? What are you on about? What year is it – what was it when you came through?"

Ivy could barely speak.

"It's been over a hundred years."

The Sinking of Mardale Green

OS Grid Ref: NY 47 11

Kit's gaze slid past Ivy and his face went blank. "Don't be ridiculous," he said quietly, and he turned and walked away, out through the kissing gate and into the lane. Grendel hesitated between them for a moment with a paw raised, then loped after Kit.

Staring after him, Ivy's brain took a moment longer than it should have to register that the sound as they walked away was not that of footsteps and paws on grass. It was splashing.

She lifted a foot and the ground squelched beneath her. The grass was covered in groundwater, like there'd been heavy rain the night before. Except that there was no weather here at all, with the cloudless not-sky looming above. And it hadn't been boggy when they'd arrived. It hadn't been boggy even a few minutes before.

Now that she looked again, only the very tips of the blades of grass stood higher than the level of the water. Its surface wasn't still, but swirling, agitated...

Ivy felt the moment it crept over the toe of her boots to the base of her shoelaces and seeped into her socks. The shock of the cold water finally jerked her into action. She raced after Kit.

He was just marching around the end of the lonning when she stepped out of the garden.

"Leave me alone!" he shouted, not looking at her, and disappeared around the bend.

"We have to stay together!" she called after him, but he didn't respond. By the time she reached the end of the lane the water had already risen over the top of her boots, making her steps drag. Kit was nowhere in sight.

Somewhere in the distance was the sound of shattering glass, and a low, uneasy rumbling that crescendoed as a building collapsed on itself. Ivy saw dust rise beyond the roofs. She waded through the water streaming down the main road, up to a dry patch on top of the humpback bridge. The river had broken its banks but not yet reached over the hump, turning it into a small island.

She climbed onto the wall of the bridge and looked around. Low Water was brimming out from the centre, waves rippling into its neighbour. High Water had risen up above the shoreline, and lakewater was racing down the narrow lanes of the village, fields becoming submerged.

She felt the rush of her body filling with adrenaline, her mind rebelling against what her eyes were telling her. The valley was flooding.

She wasn't a strong swimmer. She had a full pack.

146

And she was alone.

"KIT!" she shouted, but there was no response.

Her breath came faster and she felt it slipping out of her control, crossing into panic. She clenched and unclenched her fists as she looked frantically around the village, but her vision began to swim, a grey cloud descending. She pressed the heels of her hands to her eyes and took a deep, cleansing breath.

She needed to get higher.

Ivy jumped off the wall, sending up a spray as she splashed onto the road. The hump of the bridge was underwater now. Her hiking trousers were instantly soaked to the waist. She had to wade along the road to the nearest house, where she climbed up onto the garden wall and was momentarily above the waterline again.

Without really thinking she pulled out the map and unfolded it. They needed to get out of the valley; they needed to find their way to the nearest high ground and keep climbing.

The water was much deeper than Grendel now. Kit would be carrying him, she was sure of that. She wished fervently that she was with them.

"*KIT!*" she called again, pushing all the strength she could muster into her voice. The handprint on her arm was prickling uncomfortably, like a fresh burn. She could hear the rushing of water and splashes as pieces of the village hit the water: bricks, tiles, a chair, a boot.

But from close behind her came another sound. A

slow, hoarse release of breath that sent a shiver down her spine.

Ivy turned towards the sound and lost her balance, slipping backwards off the wall. Her pack hit the water first, taking the force of the fall, and she managed to get her legs under her before her head sank below the surface. The map had gone underwater for a moment and she hastily shook the drops off it.

But as she raised her head she saw the Spectre King standing before her, more clear and solid than he'd seemed before. The moving water parted around his ghostly form, flecked white, but no part of him looked wet. The bright eyes in his youthful face were troubled.

He lurched towards her.

Ivy waded away from him, the water pushing against her, making her unbearably slow. She didn't hear his progress behind her, but she felt the moment that cold hand closed on her shoulder. She gasped and shook herself free, leaping forwards against the water's resistance. She pushed through a gap in the garden wall and through an open door into the house, then fought against the weight of the water to push it closed behind her and slide the bolt across.

It took her a split second to realise what a terrible idea it had been to lock herself inside a house.

A hole in the roof was raining down tiles, sending great splashes up into the dark space. She pressed herself against the wall and tried to turn back.

There was a splintering sound and then a resounding

CRACK! The Spectre King pulled himself through the broken door, its rich wood now empty of colour. He advanced towards her.

"What do you want?" she cried, knowing he wouldn't answer. Ivy threw up her hands, the map clutched between them like a flimsy shield. She gasped as his hand raked through it – she felt the map tear as though it were her own heart. The force of his grasp pushed it free from her grip and down into the water.

But he wasn't trying to get the map. It drifted away on the swirling current as she met his gaze.

It was impossible to read the expression on his face. In her terror, she expected to see malice and rage in his eyes. What she saw was something more like loss.

She was pinned in the corner of a room where slates rained down like missiles and the rapidly rising water had already reached her chest. If she didn't do something, she was going to drown or be knocked unconscious or… she didn't know what the ghost king would do. But she couldn't hang around to find out.

She could whistle. Two short, sharp whistles and Taliesin could pull her out of the water, help her find Kit and Grendel, get them all to safety. All it would take was the fairy bead.

Ivy grabbed the soft, rounded stone from the pocket of her pack and closed it in her fist.

The king's eyes grew wider, brighter, and he plunged towards her. Ivy sucked in a breath and ducked under the water.

She opened her eyes at once but could see very little in the churning eddies of the rising lakewater. A dulled silver glow that must be the king. The slates slicing into the water to her left like bullets. She didn't waste a second. Ivy forced her body through the water, even as the pack weighed her down. Her searching hands found the doorway and she pulled herself through the splintered gap and up for air.

She glanced back. The king stared after her, unmoving. In the next moment he flickered and was gone.

Heaving in a breath, Ivy pulled herself along the building until she could feel the garden wall. She hauled herself onto it, and was free of the water again above her waist. Luckily the roof of the house was low, and she used the wall's cornerstones to haul herself up onto the edge. The ascent was slippery from the layer of algae, even more so with wet clothing, but she dragged herself into a sitting position, leaving her feet hanging over the drainpipe.

Ivy tucked the fairy bead still in her hand safely away. She was hardly safer here with the roof falling in on itself, but at least she was out of the water. She wouldn't be for long, though – all the stone walls were submerged now, hedges and gates vanished beneath the agitated surface of the lake. Only the tops of trees and the roofs of buildings were still above the waterline, but most of the houses were groaning and collapsing under the weight of the rising lake.

A length of frayed old rope drifted by, and Ivy stretched out at once to grab it. She almost lost her balance, but, holding tight to the drainpipe, she managed to pull it in. Quickly she wound one end around her wrist and shrugged out of her rucksack, tying the other end to one of the straps. She got unsteadily to her feet.

"KIT!" she bellowed.

For a few heartbeats, nothing. Then…

"HERE!" came the answer.

She spun around and spotted his dark curly head in a treetop a few roads away, one arm outstretched in a frantic wave. He was as high as he could get, perched at the end of a strong branch. Grendel was crouched close against him, dripping wet and looking very sorry for himself.

Ivy waved, laughing with relief. Kit waved back, a helpless grin on his face in spite of it all.

She looked out at the fells over the rapidly rising water. They needed to take action.

"SWIM TO THE FELL!" she shouted. She pointed with a broad gesture to the nearest slope. The water couldn't rise forever; once it reached the height of the reservoir, she had to hope it would stop. But not before the whole village was submerged, and them with it.

"AFTER YOU!" Kit called back.

Ivy glanced at the dark, roiling mass of water that was already lapping at her ankles. Again, she reminded herself that she had never been a strong swimmer, that she struggled enough without a full set of clothes and boots and a heavy rucksack at the end of a cord. She let the thrill of fear course through her, and then she shook her shoulders, letting it go. There was nothing else for it.

She picked up her pack and jumped.

For a heart-stopping moment she was underwater, currents rushing around her, threatening to hold her beneath the surface. She released the pack and let it float up like a buoy, then kicked hard to break the surface. As she gasped in a breath she saw Kit drop from the branch into the water, his arms around Grendel. The border collie resurfaced first, eyes white and frantically paddling. Kit appeared a moment later, panting, and gently clasped Grendel by the scruff as they began to swim.

Ivy could feel the water pushing her up and off course as she paddled towards the fell. It took all her strength to keep moving around and away from the buildings below the surface. Kit had released Grendel, who was keeping up with him as he made straight for the grassy slope in a confident front crawl.

It seemed a long way off, but the sight of Grendel's determined paddle kept Ivy moving. She tugged the rucksack after her, thankful that the sleeping bag must still be full of air. She dodged a bicycle as it came spinning through the turbulent waters towards her, then changed course sharply to stay out of range of a garden gnome racing by.

Kit hit the bank moments before she did. Immediately he turned back to help her out, and they called encouragement to Grendel as he fought the last few strokes to the shore. They clambered up the slope, panting heavily and weighed down by their soaking clothes.

At last Ivy looked back over her shoulder and realised the water had stopped rising. She tugged on Kit's arm and they collapsed together onto the grass. Grendel shook himself, showering them both in droplets that had no effect on their already soggy state. Then he too sank down onto the bank and lay flat out, his chest bouncing as he panted.

The lake was still over the drowned village of Mardale Green.

Castle Crag

OS Grid Ref: NY 46 12

Ivy lay on the bank for what felt like a very long time, letting her breathing gradually return to normal, feeling her clothes slowly begin to dry. There was no breeze to send a chill through her bones, though there was no sun to bake her dry either. A seagull drifted overhead and passed out of sight.

Ivy stared vacantly up, not really registering that she was looking at the sky for the longest uninterrupted length of time in more than a year. Because, of course, it wasn't a sky. Though her mind strayed all over the place, she absorbed what she was seeing with a kind of detachment. There were ridges and shadows, darkening shades of aubergine, mulberry, lilac. It was static and unnerving, but beautiful at the same time.

Her instinct was right: it was not a real sky; it was a roof. When she had gone through the wall, she had gone down too, beneath the stone. Underfell. *Under the fells…*

Thinking of skies and not-skies gave her the urge to

154

reach for her map and check their position. She sat up abruptly and towed her pack in at the end of the rope, but before it reached her, she remembered the sound of tearing and the shredded paper floating away. Fresh pain struck her.

"I lost the map," Ivy said in barely more than a whisper. "It's gone."

She glanced at Kit. He was flat on his back, arms spread, staring blankly up.

"Do you know what fell this is?" she asked. "Do you know where we are?"

She thought that he hadn't heard her; his face didn't even flicker. But then he said, "Rough Crag." His voice betrayed nothing. He still didn't look her way.

Ivy pulled her legs to her chest and wrapped her arms tightly around them. She rested her chin on her knees, trying to breathe deliberately, evenly. Determined not to see the greyness, like static, that flickered in her peripheral vision when she thought about the map.

When Kit finally spoke, it came out as a croak. "Mardale Green is gone. My house. It's gone."

Ivy blinked and turned to him, momentarily forgetting.

"This isn't the real Mardale Green," she reminded him. "It's—"

"I know that!" he shot back, sitting up and meeting her gaze. "I'm not talking about this place." He glanced at the reservoir with a curled lip. "It's been over a hundred years. There is no Mardale Green any more.

You'd never even heard of it! And what does that mean for my parents? For me? For Billy? Are they all gone? What am I going—"

He stopped suddenly, but Ivy heard the rest of the question. *What am I going back to?*

The silence lingered. Another question hung in the air, unspoken by either of them.

Was he going back at all?

It had already been more than a century since Kit had entered Underfell.

How long would it have been by the time they got home?

Ivy felt that terrible ache in her wrists and forearms again. She couldn't contemplate the notion of being stuck in Underfell forever.

"I need to find King Eveling," Kit said firmly, not looking at her. "I'm going to find him and ask for my wish, and get him to take me to Billy."

"What about—" Ivy began at once, but Kit cut across her.

"Callum? Everything is about you and Callum, isn't it? There's nowt stopping you from coming with me and asking Eveling too, Ivy!" He didn't try to hide the frustration in his voice. "I can't just keep following you."

The last words hit Ivy like a blow to the chest. "We're looking together," she said in a small voice.

Her vision blurred as she tried to process what he was saying, but then her eyes sharpened again and she found herself looking at the squat, slate-grey tower they had first noticed on approach to Mardale Green.

Keep clear of the hermit on Castle Crag, Taliesin had told them. But Taliesin had sent them here, to Mardale Green, to a sinking village. His word wasn't good for much.

From where Ivy was sitting, she could pick out several small shapes soaring in the sky over the tower. They were birds, their silhouettes fast, sharp and brutal.

Birds of prey.

"Are you even listening to me?" she heard Kit saying, and she snapped back to attention. He had been speaking all this time and she hadn't heard a word he'd said.

"Look." She pointed to the tower. "There are birds of prey there! They might have kestrels. They might have seen Callum! We could just take a look. Please, stay with me." She hated the imploring tone in her voice. "We can go to Eveling together, after—"

"After you've found Callum," Kit supplied, and there was a dreadful, dull finality to his words. "I mean it, Ivy. I can't keep following you around, waiting until you've found your brother so we can finally look for mine. I'm going to Eveling. You should come with me."

"But what are you going to give him?" Ivy pressed. "We don't have anything we could trade for a wish."

"Yes, we do." His eyes flicked to her pack and he swallowed. "We could give him the fairy bead."

Ivy placed a protective hand on her rucksack at once, anger boiling up inside her. "No." She couldn't believe he would suggest such a thing.

"It's obviously worth something if Taliesin wants it so

badly!" Kit shot back. "You said yourself you can't make it do anything, so at least we can use it for this. We can trade it for both of them." She thought she saw a flicker of pleading cross his face, but it vanished as quickly as it had come.

"We don't know that Eveling is even real! Have you heard anyone mention his name since we got here? All you know are your nan's stories. Callum is a kestrel and there are birds of prey right there that for some reason Taliesin doesn't want us to know about. There is no way I'm traipsing back through Underfell chasing a fairy story when Billy has already been gone for a century and Callum's running out of time."

They just stared at each other for a few unsteady seconds. Ivy regretted her words the moment they passed her lips, but she didn't take them back.

It dawned on her, with deepening dread, that she was not going to persuade Kit.

He looked away from her, shaking his head as if to clear it, and got to his feet. "I have to go."

She stood as well, putting herself between him and the pack, but he didn't make a move for it.

Kit whistled. "Come, Grendel." The collie leapt to his feet and trotted to Kit's side as he turned and began to stride away. That hurt more than anything. Ivy clutched her damp T-shirt close, watching as her only friends in this unknown place left her behind.

"But you don't have a map!" she called helplessly after them.

Kit spared her a glance over his shoulder and the corner of his mouth quirked. It wasn't a smile.

Ivy felt the grey fog threatening, felt her heart picking up speed, her knees wanting to give way. Alone. Alone in the fells.

She took deep, steadying breaths and hardened her anxiety into resolve. She felt the ground, solid and unwavering, beneath her boots. She heard the sing-song of birds flitting overhead. She turned her back on the boy and the dog leaving her behind, picked up her pack and tugged it on. Then she left *them* behind and marched away towards the tower.

She didn't look back.

"Wood. Woooooood."

Ivy awoke from her doze with a start, wondering where the voice had come from. She was tucked beneath a rocky overhang at the foot of a high crag; beyond her shaded spot, the valley was still flooded with light. She glanced around with an embarrassing rush of hope, but it was immediately clear that she was still alone.

"Hello?" she ventured anyway.

A wood pigeon cooed softly from the wrinkled branch of a hawthorn tree on the slope just outside her cave. It cocked its periwinkle-blue head at her and shifted from foot to foot.

"Oh. Hello." Ivy let out a deep sigh. She scanned the

valley beyond the crag, realising as she did so that she was half-expecting Kit and Grendel to be making their way towards her, tails between their legs. But deep down she knew they weren't coming back.

She had lost her only friends.

Her stomach growled and she was suddenly aware of how long it had been since her last meal. She dug through the pack – everything inside it was damp. Fortunately, the container of trail mix was still sealed and its contents unharmed. She tore off the lid and gobbled up the last of the chocolate and cashews.

She was out of food. She had to make it a priority to find some more, and soon. Tucking the container away again, she looked mournfully at the bag of pink dog kibble that the others had left behind. Grendel would have to fend for himself again.

She pulled out her binoculars. The hard leather case had protected them for the most part, but there was still some water on the lenses. She cleaned them carefully and slung the strap over her head. Peering through the eyepieces, she scanned the ground until she found the base of the tower, grey stone springing from green grass, and followed its outline up. It seemed the flurry of activity she had witnessed earlier was over now, for the tower and the sky above it were quiet and still.

Ivy dropped the binoculars and sat back, leaning against the smooth stone. She folded her hands in her lap and waited, trying not to think about Kit and Grendel. It wasn't much longer before her patience was rewarded by the distant sound of a door closing. Ivy crept forwards immediately, lifting the binoculars to her eyes. A figure was emerging from the tower.

She was a human woman, with tawny skin and long, straight black hair that cascaded down over a waxy green coat with a fur trim. She was short but broad and strong, with worn leather boots whose heavy steps Ivy could hear even from where she perched. Most interesting of all: on one arm she wore a leather glove the colour of polished wood, with panels of tan in a swirling pattern surrounding the shape of a bird in flight. And on that arm, held firmly by a length of cord wound through a brass ring on the glove itself, perched a bird.

It had strong legs set wide apart, striking wings and a long tail like a dart down its back. Its feathers were cream with paint dabs of bark-brown, its eyes golden, its beak short and curving to a lethal point.

A goshawk.

With one hand, the falconer untied the bird. She raised her arm and it flapped up into the sky. Ivy followed its flight, enraptured. Then she moved her gaze down to the woman as she unwound a long rope and attached something to the end.

This was the unfriendly hermit Taliesin had warned them about?

Holding the rope in two hands, the falconer began to swing it around over her head. Ivy remembered when Iona had taken her and Callum to see a falconry display at the county show. This was called a lure, and it was something to do with training the bird.

Ivy watched in awe as the goshawk dove for the lure and the falconer swung it out of the bird's reach, over and over. Finally, the bird was allowed to ensnare its prey and the lure fell heavily to the ground. The goshawk's wings spread wide to shield its kill as it tore into whatever tasty morsel had been attached to it.

There was a sudden cry from above. Ivy saw through the binoculars that both hawk and falconer looked up sharply at the sound, and she followed their gazes until she found the object of their interest.

A honey buzzard was soaring high overhead, with wings the colour of ginger biscuits dipped in cream and chocolate. It called again, a piercing, drawn-out whistle. There were no leather straps on its legs, like the goshawk had. It was a wild bird.

When Ivy glanced down, she was interested to see that the falconer had the goshawk on her arm again and was transferring it to a wooden perch set into the wall of the tower. The woman tied the cord to a ring on the perch and said something gentle to the bird that Ivy couldn't hear, then turned away and tilted her face up to the not-sky.

Ivy took a quick look up into the violet and saw the buzzard moving further away, though it still scanned every part of the ground, including the falconer and – she thought – herself.

Then the falconer did a very curious thing. She raised her arm as though the great raptor were tame and would fly straight to it. The bird-shaped panel on the falconer's glove began to glow. It was golden and bright, like a lit sparkler. It crackled and whirled.

And the buzzard changed direction.

It was nothing dramatic. With a simple pitch to one side, the buzzard's course changed. Gradually it arced around until it was heading back towards the tower. The goshawk began to cry and shift on its perch as the golden bird soared down like an arrow towards them. Then, as if it had been trained all its life, the buzzard threw its body back and buffered its wings on the air, coming in to land lightly on the falconer's glove.

The golden crackling dimmed to a dull glow as the falconer lowered her arm. Ivy watched as she checked the bird from head to foot, stretching out a wing and examining it, looking closely at the beak and claws. When her examination was complete she nodded, said something unintelligible to the creature, and raised her arm again.

The buzzard took off, flapping back up into the not-sky as though nothing out of the ordinary had happened.

But Ivy's eyes remained fixed on the ground – on the magical leather glove that had enabled the falconer to summon a wild bird straight to her hand.

I need that glove, she thought to herself.

The Falconer's Glove

OS Grid Ref: NY 46 12

Ivy waited until long after dark. She sat beneath the crag and watched through the binoculars as the falconer went about her evening: bringing in clothes from the washing line, fetching wood from the woodpile, walking down to the stream and returning with full buckets of water that sloshed with each step. The last thing she did was fly another of the birds – a merlin, Ivy thought. Then she disappeared into the tower and didn't return. Within what felt like minutes, it was dark.

The tower wall was pocked with slits too narrow to be called windows; Ivy thought they might have been for firing arrows out at invaders. The tower was certainly in a good position to defend, overlooking the valley with the mountains at its back. When darkness had descended, she could see the warm glow of candlelight through those gaps in the stonework.

Eventually, the light went out. Ivy's immediate instinct was to jump up and run down the slope, but she checked herself. It would be silly to make her move too quickly. She needed to wait until the falconer was so deeply asleep she wouldn't be easily disturbed.

She gave it an hour, or what she thought was about an hour.

When the time came, she felt strange. She wished she had someone to run her plan by, to exercise her voice. It had felt like a very quiet afternoon without Kit's tuneless whistling and his one-sided conversations with Grendel.

She felt a stab of loss, then got to her feet.

Ivy pulled on her pack, because she wasn't planning to come back up here once the job was done. She put her head torch in place and switched it onto a dim setting: just enough light to see by, but not so bright that she'd draw attention to herself. Hopefully.

She set off towards the tower, picking her way down the rocky slope with care. She had made sure to have a good look at the going before the light disappeared, since it was steep and uncertain and she could easily picture herself falling head over heels in the darkness. She kept her beam fixed on the ground so that the light wouldn't flash through the arrowslits.

On the approach to the tower she trod as lightly as she could. The grass was not damp with dew as it would be back home; it was like moving through a warm summer's night. Somewhere in the darkness, a nightjar trilled.

When she was no more than a metre away from the thick stone wall Ivy paused and listened. No sound reached her from within, but her own heartbeats were loud in her chest. She approached the door.

It took her a few moments to persuade herself to touch the iron door handle. She wrapped her hand around it and turned, gently at first, then harder when nothing clicked. It was no good; the door was locked.

Ivy felt the immediate urge to give up. It wasn't meant to be; she'd find Callum some other way. Maybe it wasn't too late to track down Kit and Grendel, go with them to Eveling and make her wish.

But that chance had come and gone. Instead, she adjusted the angle of her head torch and scanned slowly up the grey façade.

Not far above her, there was an arrowslit. Now that she was beside the wall, Ivy saw that it wasn't as narrow as she'd thought from afar. In fact, it looked just wide enough for a thirteen-year-old girl to fit through.

She peered closely at the wall itself, the stones it was made from. It was an ancient structure, of that much she was sure. She was almost certain there had been no tower on the crag when she'd come canoeing at Haweswater before, which meant that it must be a ruin now, up above. The stones were fitted together in a higgledy-piggledy way; there were places where she could rest a toe or a hand.

She could climb it.

She shrugged off her backpack and left it on the grass. Then she stood up close to the wall so that she was staring right into its blank grey face and wished again that Kit were with her, after his stories about bouldering with Billy. She enjoyed scrambling up crags that crossed her path, but she wasn't a climber – there was a big difference.

Ivy tucked her fingers into the ridges between stones, lifted her feet to the wall and began to climb.

Her breathing felt very loud by the time she reached the arrowslit. Quickly she switched off the torch and tucked her hands into the gap to hold herself firmly to the wall. She gave herself a moment to catch her breath and allow her eyes to adapt to the darkness.

If only Callum could see her now.

She peered through the arrowslit into the tower's interior, but all was pitch black. The only thing she could make out was the faint light of the bioluminescence outside leaking through the other arrowslits. It gave her a rough sense of the size of the tower, and she could see that it was all one large room. As her vision grew sharper still, she saw the reflection of the light on stone within – a staircase that seemed to wind around the whole tower from bottom to top.

Ivy took a deep breath, adjusted her feet and heaved herself up into the gap. She was right – she could fit through it, but only if she pivoted her body sideways. She worked her arms through and took hold of the inside of the window, then stuck one leg in, followed by the other. She levered her upper body through until her legs were dangling over nothing but air on the other side. Then she twisted herself until her feet found purchase on the interior wall.

The muscles in her forearms began to protest at once. On this side the wall sloped away from her, and she wasn't strong enough to hold on. But she could drop. The arrowslit hadn't been much higher than her head. It wasn't that far to fall... but she didn't know what was at the bottom.

Ivy held her breath and let go.

Her feet hit the ground with a thump and the breath whooshed out of her. It really hadn't been that far, and she had landed on something soft and loose that smelled distinctly like straw.

She reached out with a hand to feel her surroundings. The cold wall was right in front of her, and to her side what felt like a wooden post... and then...

"Ouch!" she hissed, snatching her hand back.

Her night vision had sharpened further. She found herself staring into the sharp eyes of a small, agitated bird whose perch she had been blindly exploring. She took a step backwards, holding up her hands apologetically.

A long, loud snore made Ivy jump. It was followed by the smacking of lips, a mumbled word, and then another snore. She tilted her head back, following her ears to the source of the sound.

Holding her breath, she switched her head torch back on to the dimmest setting. At the top of the tower was a stone platform, over the edge of which she could just see a hand and the fringe of some animal pelts. She froze in alarm, but the hand didn't move and the snoring continued. The falconer was asleep.

The stairs wound from the platform around the edge of the tower, down in a spiral to ground level. As Ivy followed its curve with her eyes, she saw that there were perches set into the wall beside the stairs at equal distances, four in total. Each was occupied; some of the birds were deeply asleep, while others shifted and eyed Ivy's light suspiciously.

At the foot of the stairs was the smallest raptor, right beside Ivy; in the faint light of the head torch, she realised that it was the merlin the falconer had been flying earlier. It was still staring angrily at her.

Then it opened its beak and screeched.

Ivy ran backwards, thinking quickly. She scoured the room with her torch beam, searching for anything to distract it. Hanging from a nail on the wall she laid eyes on the pouch that the falconer had worn earlier that day. She ran up to it and pulled it down, flipping open the leather flap.

Quickly she pulled one of the small, wet chunks of meat out of the pouch and tossed it to the merlin. As though they had rehearsed it, the bird snatched the meat out of the air, then took it into its claws and began to tear chunks off.

Ivy glanced up at the platform above. There was silence for a few heart-stopping moments – then another snore punctured the quiet.

She breathed a sigh of relief, slung the pouch over her shoulder and took the time to slowly scan the room again. It was sparsely furnished: a low table with a few scattered cushions on the floor, a shelf of books, pots and pans around a wood-burning stove, tools and falconry equipment hanging from hooks on the walls. It was surprisingly cosy, really.

But she wasn't here to admire the falconer's interior decorating. The glove didn't seem to be hanging from the wall, but there were a couple of chests beside the bookshelf. Ivy crept over to them and gently lifted each lid in turn, rifling through the contents. There were a number of ordinary leather falconry gloves, but she knew at once they weren't the right ones. They didn't have the design of the bird in flight, and they weren't the rich colours of the glove she had seen the falconer using earlier.

Only when she was absolutely certain that the glove was nowhere to be found on the ground floor did she turn her gaze to the stairs.

It had to be with the falconer.

Ivy wanted so badly not to have to climb those stairs and creep around that sleeping figure. But this was Callum. This was the best chance she had of finding him. There was nothing else for it.

She turned off her torch again, now that her eyes were fairly well adjusted to the darkness. She could distinctly see the outline of the steps now, the birds stationed along the wall.

She started to climb. Keeping one hand ready in the pouch, at every perch she dug out a piece of meat and flung it to the bird. They were all awake and shifting now, but remained mercifully quiet as she passed and were quickly appeased by her offerings. She saw the goshawk again; a barn owl, whose beautiful colouring she couldn't fully appreciate in the darkness; and a curious red kite. Their sharp beaks tore through the food she threw them like tissue paper, their powerful claws locked like vices around their perches. On any other occasion, she would have slowed down and soaked in every second.

But now wasn't the time.

When Ivy finally reached the platform she was practically shaking. The falconer lay sprawled on a pile of furs, covered with what looked like a grey wolf's pelt. Her mouth hung open as she snored; up close, she was much younger than Ivy had imagined.

No one looked intimidating while sleeping, Ivy supposed, feeling somewhat relieved. She waited without moving for a moment to allow her heart to settle back to a steady drum.

Then her eyes strayed to the glove – and her heart leapt into a gallop again.

It was lying on the ground between the falconer's head and a bed of straw. Ivy lifted her eyes and had to bite back a yelp of fright.

Huge clawed feet gripped a great branch bolted into the wall. The colossal bird had to be half a metre tall at least, standing guard over the falconer while she slept. Ivy felt its eyes on her, and then it adjusted its feet and threw out its enormous wings, showing her the blinding white feathers underneath, reflecting back what little light the room offered.

An osprey.

It seemed too wild, too strange, an impossible animal to partner with.

Hurriedly she pulled a hunk of meat from the pouch and tossed it to the bird. It hit the ground with a small thump. The bird didn't even flinch.

Ivy's eyes widened. The osprey's gaze was fixed on her, unmoving.

And then it shrieked.

The falconer started at once, rolling over in her sleep and making some unintelligible sound.

Ivy didn't hesitate. She leapt forwards, swept up the glove and turned to run.

She was jerked back. The strap of the leather pouch had caught on the osprey's perch, and she flailed to get away from it as the bird screeched again. She pulled until she heard a snap and then threw the pouch off her shoulders anyway, stumbling forwards with the sudden release of pressure.

The falconer was sitting up, still half-asleep. Ivy glanced over her shoulder as she flung herself down the stairs and caught the woman's eye.

Suddenly the falconer was wide awake. "OI!" she shouted after Ivy, her voice echoing around the room.

Ivy took the stairs three at a time, letting gravity carry her down to the foot of the tower. There was a whoosh overhead and she ducked, heart pounding, as something brushed through her hair.

She had broken the straps that kept the osprey

tethered. It was loose.

"STOP!" came the falconer's voice again, and her footsteps thundered down the staircase in Ivy's wake. But Ivy was already at the foot of the stairs. She found the door, fumbled until she found a bolt and slid it across.

She stumbled out into the night, scrambling for the straps of her backpack propped beside the door. A gust of air almost knocked her off her feet as the osprey swooped over her head again. She reached up to knock it away, but the bird wasn't interested in her; it was already soaring up and away. Behind her, the falconer was shouting something she couldn't hear because her heart was pounding too loudly in her ears.

Ivy staggered to her feet and tore into the darkness.

Ivy Adrift

OS Grid Ref: NY 49 20

Birds of prey were screeching and circling overhead, and Ivy North was crouched under the trees, trying desperately to hold her breath and stay silent while her body fought to pant. With one hand, she held the enchanted glove tightly against her chest. In the other, she clutched one strap of her backpack, dusty and torn from her rush through the undergrowth.

She had to breathe. She allowed herself a few sharp gasps, and the air felt like a glass of water after a long, hot day. But then she quieted herself again and listened. The birds were still noisy overhead. They were looking for her.

She had to keep moving – before one of them found her and alerted the falconer.

Ivy hefted her backpack onto her shoulders and adjusted the straps until it sat snugly against her back. She took another few gulps of air, relieved to find that her breathing was finally settling, then set off walking.

It was dark. She had no map. She had no bearing

on where she was, except that she was in the vicinity of Haweswater.

She kept walking.

She kept to the cover of trees, kept her head torch beam switched off, kept her gaze focused on the not-sky between the branches in search of a darker shape silhouetted against the glittering spray of bioluminescence. Her ears ached with the strain of listening out for the calls of a kite, an osprey, a goshawk, a merlin…

The barn owl, with its sharp night eyes, worried her most of all.

Ivy waited to hear that banshee cry, for the falconer to come crashing through the undergrowth. But the sounds of the birds in flight were soon lost altogether as she travelled further and further from the tower. Towards what, she wasn't sure.

She walked through the night, too frightened to do anything but keep moving.

Sometimes she thought about Kit and Grendel, wondering where they were at that moment, whether they had found Eveling already and were being welcomed into his court. Whether she had made a terrible mistake.

Ivy cut those thoughts off quickly.

She stumbled on until her legs grew weak with exhaustion, and then she kept going, following the curves of hills she didn't know the names of, letting her feet and gravity guide her up and back down again. Each time she emerged from a stand of trees she frowned into the night until she picked out the dark blot of the next patch of woodland and darted towards it.

The moment the light came up, she collapsed onto the ground.

She found herself on the edge of a wintry larch wood, the trees tall and spaced apart, violet light filtering between their skeletal branches. Never had Ivy been so happy to see that strange lavender glow, though maybe *happy* wasn't quite the right word. She was relieved to have left the falconer far behind, exhausted from everything that had happened in the past few days, and when she allowed herself to look deeper, she found a bubbling turmoil of anxiety and fear.

But she had the glove.

When she had recovered enough that her legs could bear the weight of her body, when she had inhaled the scent of larch needles until her mind felt clear again, Ivy got to her feet.

She examined the glove closely, but though it was soft and supple and very beautiful to look at, there was nothing to indicate it was anything more than a regular falconry glove. There were no magic words stitched into the leather. There was no switch to flick.

For the first time it occurred to her that the glove may just be a glove, that the falconer might be a witch, or part-fairy, that the magic might have flowed from her. The very idea made Ivy dig her nails into her palms. She had the glove now, and it had to work. It had to.

Ivy slipped it onto her hand and up her arm. It wasn't

a perfect fit, but it didn't need to be.

She knew what to do next, but she found her gaze was fixed on the ground beneath her feet, grass peeking out between fallen larch needles – not beaten to dust by many pairs of boots before her, not waymarked. She was adrift, without a path to guide her.

She pushed this thought away and steeled herself, raised her arm ready to receive the weight of a bird, and scanned the sky.

"Callum!" she called, but her vision quickly clouded with grey and she had to drop her head. Ivy took a deep, even breath and forced herself to lift her gaze again.

"CALLUM!" she shouted, scanning from one end of the horizon to the other.

Nothing happened. She brought the glove in close, checking the panel of the bird in flight. There was only the faintest hint of a glow in the deeply etched lines.

She tried again, raising her arm. "*Caaaaaaaaaaalluuuuuuuuuuuuuum!*" she called, as if by drawing out his name she had a better chance of catching his attention.

Ivy waited, her chest tight with the desperate wish to see her kestrel-brother come winging down out of the violet sky to rest on her arm. Even if he was a bird, at least they could figure it out together. At least she wouldn't be alone.

The glove's glow grew momentarily stronger, sparkled just the tiniest bit, then guttered and faded to nothing.

There was no answer.

She cast her mind back to what she had witnessed on Castle Crag. The falconer had seen the buzzard flying by, and then all she'd had to do was lift her arm and the glove had burned to life.

She had *seen* the bird…

Ivy felt her shoulders droop as the weight of the realisation sunk in. The glove couldn't bring her a bird that was nowhere in sight.

If she found Callum, she had a way to catch him…

But she still had to find him first.

Ivy's stomach was complaining loudly by the time she opened her eyes. She found herself curled into a ball at the foot of a tree, on a soft bed of larch needles.

The world was grey. It was hardly worth opening her eyes at all, because the thin ice of calm she had been treading on through Underfell was cracked. She was far from home and had lost her map; Kit and Grendel were gone; and she was no closer to finding Callum than she'd been when she'd first set foot here. If the Spectre King came upon her now, she didn't see how she could face him alone.

She squeezed her eyes shut against the haze, feeling dizzy.

Why hadn't she seen the slightest trace of her brother? She had travelled all over Underfell without glimpsing so much as a feather. If he wasn't out looking for her, maybe…

If Callum was still Callum – and that was an 'if' that made her chest clench – maybe he was waiting for her somewhere. Somewhere significant to both of them. Somewhere she would know to look for him. It was the beginning of a plan. But how would she ever get there?

And that was assuming he wasn't as lost as she was.

That was assuming he still knew *who* he was.

"HEART!" came a sudden cry. Ivy shot bolt upright, clutching the straps of her backpack.

"Who's there?" she called, surprising herself to find that she no longer cared who heard her.

"Heart!" the voice answered.

The call was like a bell, but Ivy couldn't have said where it came from. She looked all around, but there was no one in sight, nothing moving but the ever-present birds overhead. A seagull was perched on a high branch of the tree she was sitting under, a flock of sparrows were chasing each other from one tree to another, and a couple of hawfinches were eyeing her beadily from the low branches of a nearby shrub.

"Who said that?" she asked again. There was no answer.

But the hawfinches had got her thinking.

She did have one option left to her.

Ivy wobbled to her feet, brushing needles off her trousers. She adjusted the weight of her backpack and sighed. Then she whistled. Two short, sharp chirps.

The hawfinches cocked their heads and took wing. Ivy watched them disappear into the trees. If they were delivering her message themselves, how long would it take for them to reach Taliesin and bring him back to her?

"Ivy. You've reconsidered."

She flinched. Taliesin's voice was as smooth as spider's silk, and it sent a chill down her spine as she turned to face him. Today he was dressed in a hunter-green tweed suit over a white shirt patterned with red squirrels. Maybe it was the light of day, but he looked somehow older than when they had met in the tea rooms. There was a heaviness to his brow and dark smudges beneath his eyes, as though he hadn't been sleeping.

Ivy's stomach growled again. She already knew she was covered in dirt, her clothes were creased and stale from her dip in the reservoir, and her hair felt like what Iona would call a bird's nest. She was beyond embarrassment. "What have you got to eat?" she asked.

Taliesin's expression lightened for the merest moment. "You want to trade the fairy bead for food?" he said, a laugh in his voice. "I must say, I didn't predict that."

"Not to trade. I just can't do business on an empty stomach," Ivy replied.

Taliesin narrowed his eyes at her, weighing her words, then tutted impatiently and began to pat down the pockets of his suit.

"But I need to know if you were telling the truth about fairy food first," Ivy added quickly. "Will it trap me here?"

"It wasn't a lie." His tone was weary. "We really have no desire to keep humans around." He dug something out of the inside breast pocket of his tweed jacket and held it out.

Ivy tried to read the truth in his face, but it was too difficult to decipher. She would be no help to Callum on an empty stomach, so she took it from him.

"What is it?" She unfolded the colourful beeswax wrapping.

"Bread," Taliesin replied.

In her palm was a round, flat bun, glistening like it was coated in sugar. It didn't look much like bread to Ivy, more like cake. It was hardly bigger than a conker.

"Not like human bread, mind you," Taliesin went on. "It'll fill you up much longer than that rubbish. Fairies have very long lives, you see, and we can't afford to be cooking for ourselves three times a day. Imagine the loss of productivity."

Ivy lifted the bun out of its wrapping, sniffed it – it smelled sugary, too – and popped it into her mouth. It was sweet, doughy and delicious. The moment she swallowed, the angry voice in her stomach went silent. In fact, she felt as though she would never need to eat again.

"Thanks," she said reluctantly.

"If you're finished," Taliesin said, and Ivy noticed he was tapping the toe of his shiny leather shoe.

She licked her fingers clean and wiped them dry on her trousers. "I'm done."

"Your circumstances have changed, I take it." He pointedly surveyed the empty space around her. He may as well have shouted *YOUR FRIENDS LEFT YOU!*

It stung, but she tried not to let it show. In that moment she didn't care about the ways he tried to put her down or intimidate her. She had very little left to lose. Ivy drew herself up and mimicked his businesslike tone. "Somewhat."

Her attitude seemed to take him aback, but he just adjusted the cuffs of his shirt. "What are the terms of the trade?" he asked. "They must be settled before we make the exchange."

"I need a map." It was the one thing that could get her back on track.

Taliesin's eyebrows lifted the barest fraction. "And in return?"

She avoided his gaze as she answered, "I'll give you the fairy bead."

She felt rather than saw the grin spread across his face, as she was still studiously avoiding meeting his eyes. He stuck out his hand, and there seemed to be nothing to do but take it. His grip was firm, his hand cold.

But he held onto her hand a moment too long, angling her arm so that the silver handprint shimmered between them both. "Where did you come by this, Ivy?"

She saw that his face had clouded again and shook herself free, stepping back to her rucksack. The question unnerved her. Taliesin knew something about the Spectre King, but he couldn't have deliberately set the ghost after her if he was surprised to see the handprint. How was he connected to it all?

"You know, I don't remember."

He didn't press the matter.

Ivy dug into the rucksack's side pocket, feeling a flash of panic as she did so that she was making the wrong decision, that she needed the bead and only Callum knew why – but she had no choice—

The bead wasn't there.

She must have switched it to the other pocket at some point.

She dug around. It wasn't there either.

Ivy risked a glance at Taliesin and saw his face crumpled with concern. She opened up the main compartment of the pack and began to dig through it. Her searching fingers found nothing resembling a small, smooth, spherical stone. She started pulling objects out until the whole bag was empty, even tipped it upside down.

The fairy bead was gone.

Taliesin stared at her with unconcealed dismay as she crouched in the wreckage of her belongings. Her stomach churned with mingled confusion and panic.

"I'm sorry," she heard herself say. "It's not…"

When he didn't move, she started to shove everything back in – her tent and sleeping bag, her clothes, her camping gear… No order, no method, just stuffed in willy-nilly while she worked out what to do next.

Finally, only the enchanted falconry glove lay between them on the grass, and Taliesin seemed to notice it in the same moment she did. His eyes boggled.

He knew what it was.

"Now where did you get that?" he asked softly, but

clearly he didn't expect a response. He knew of the falconer, so it stood to reason that he knew exactly where she had obtained it.

The air suddenly felt thick with tension. Ivy swallowed.

Taliesin had already begun to hum, and he reached out his hand in the same instant that she leapt for the glove. She got there first and clutched it to her chest, though it strained as if it was trying to get free.

Taliesin faltered and dropped the spell; the glove stopped wriggling. He adjusted his suit jacket, and his gaze was cold as he met Ivy's eyes. "Give that to me now, Ivy," he said. "Your brother stole from me; you lied to me; now you've made a bargain you can't keep. I'll catch Callum myself and he can tell me where the bead is."

"You aren't going anywhere near him!" Ivy spat, surprising herself. "I'm telling you, he doesn't have the bead either. I don't know where it is. I'll use this to find him and we'll leave Underfell. The deal's off. There's no need for you to bother us any more."

Taliesin's jaw clenched. He shook his head slowly. "That just won't do." His wings, always tucked politely behind his shoulders, began to unfold. They spread out to their full wingspan, casting her in shadow.

He lunged. She took a step backwards and her heel caught on a knotted root and sent her sprawling. But before Taliesin could snatch the glove from her grasp, there was a rush of air and noise as a flock of shrieking birds descended upon them.

184

Ivy ducked her head under her arms, but not a single bird came for her. A whirlwind of grey and white had enveloped Taliesin, who struggled to break free of the flock as orange beaks pecked at his hands and face and strong wings beat him back.

Seagulls.

Seagulls were holding Taliesin back, giving Ivy a chance to escape.

She didn't waste a second. She ran.

Mayburgh Henge

OS Grid Ref: NY 51 28

It was the second time in less than a day that Ivy had fled in fear, but this time she didn't have darkness to shield her. The pounding of her feet quickly took her out of sight of Taliesin and his plague of seagulls, but in her hurry to put distance between them she took no notice of her surroundings. She just kept her head down and kept moving, letting her trusty hiking boots eat up the ground, diving beneath gorse and rowan whenever birds or fairies passed overhead.

She was racing over a blank, unyielding landscape. Not a single path unveiled itself to her. In the light of day it was harder to fight her fears as she crossed the unmarked land, the certainty that she was lost beyond help. She kept stumbling onwards, but greyness crept in at the edges of her vision and threatened to engulf it.

The birdsong around her had risen to a cacophony again and winged creatures darted between bushes and branches as she passed. But through the birds' ceaseless chirping she began to discern a steady drone, and it seemed to be growing louder.

Checking over her shoulder to make certain Taliesin hadn't caught up to her, Ivy ran up to the crest of a hill and peered down into the next valley.

There was a river. The gully was densely forested and she could only pick out flickers of fast-flowing water between the crowns of the trees. But the sound of rushing water was unmistakable. It was music to her ears.

Ivy ran down the grassy slope in small, quick steps as gravity tried to carry her faster, jolting her knees. She reached out a hand to brush the bark of a tree as she moved into the forested ravine and the rush of the river finally overtook the noise of birds. She stepped up to the bank.

She didn't know which river it was, but if she followed it downstream she might reach a larger river she recognised, or a settlement, or the sea. At least then she could begin to work out where she was. She may not have a map, but it was a path, of sorts.

Ivy refilled her bottle from a little waterfall, drank it to the dregs and filled it again. Then she tucked it away in her pack and set off.

As she walked along the bank beside the steadily flowing water, Ivy realised that her heart had been pounding for so long that her whole chest was aching. It was receding now, quietening down to a calm beat. There was still a tinge of grey to the world, and her mind felt like an overcrowded nest, but her panic was easing. There was no sign of Taliesin, and she began to believe she had evaded him, for now.

After some time the trees began to thin out, until finally she was walking alongside a wide, open river surrounded by wildflowers, with grassy farmland on the far bank. Up ahead, she saw the glint of light on the surface of another river, running almost parallel to the one she was following. The two were about to meet and flow together.

Then, through the meadow of wildflowers, a peculiar curve to the earth caught her eye: a kind of hill that looked almost natural, but somehow jarred, like a trick of the light.

It was man-made. An earthwork.

It was familiar.

Ivy's heart leapt. Without a moment's hesitation, she ran towards the mound. It expanded as she drew closer until it filled her vision, and when she reached it she scrambled up the bank, fingers digging into the turf to heave herself onto the curve of its crest.

She was standing on the edge of a wide, doughnut-shaped embankment. Now that her feet had purchase, she could feel that it was constructed of stones and earth, carpeted with grass over the course of centuries. Trees had sprouted from the bank and grown to their full height at unlikely angles.

In two places there were openings in the mound, with huge stones standing sentinel at either side like gateposts. But there was one other, standing tall in the centre of the circle. From where she stood it looked twice as tall as she was, leaning heavily to one side, its faces wrinkled and grey.

This was Mayburgh Henge. She had been here before, of course, or the version of it that existed in the world above. Iona had brought them a couple of years ago, on Callum's birthday. He loved nothing better than to visit the biggest, strangest, most unlikely stones in the county. This could easily be one of the places he might choose to wait for her.

"Callum?" she called. "CALLUM!"

She peered up at the not-sky, but it was empty. Everything seemed still inside the henge; even the birds were muted.

Ivy slid down the bank into the circle, letting the quiet wash over her. She walked up to the standing stone until it dwarfed her, staring at its rough surface. How old was this stone? How long had it stood here?

She sat down with her back against it and gazed around the earthwork, scanning the tree branches, the monoliths. She tried not to let disappointment overwhelm her. If only he had been waiting, perched on top of this stone...

How long had she been in Underfell? She was losing track of the days. For all she knew, Callum had forgotten her by now. What if, after all this, she found him too late? What was she supposed to do then?

She pictured herself going back through the wall

without Callum, trying to explain to her mum that he was gone and would never be coming back. She let out a sob.

In the quiet, the sound startled her, and she swallowed and took a deep breath. There were other places he might be, and she could start by searching those.

But she had lost her map. She may know where she was now, but how long would it be before she lost her way again? She wouldn't make it much further than the next valley without panicking. The knowledge made her heart heavy. Maybe if Kit and Grendel had still been with her, they could have worked it out together. Kit never seemed to let anything knock him down.

But she had messed that up too, hadn't she?

"Ivy." A voice drifted over to her, carrying her name, warm with welcome.

Ivy jumped at the sound. She leapt to her feet, dashing away the tears from her cheeks with the back of her hand.

She moved around the stone and saw that, from the other side of the henge, a woman was approaching. Another human! She was fair-skinned, with a thick silver-grey braid that swung with each step, and a friendly, open face with smile lines around her eyes.

"Hello," Ivy said in an effort to be polite, before adding, "Do I know you?"

The woman laughed as she stopped before her, then held out a hand. It was warm and firm in Ivy's grasp as they shook. "Bega," she introduced herself.

"Oh," said Ivy, unsure how to respond. Could it really be? The Irish princess from Kit's story?

She was saved from her hesitancy by a seagull who soared down from the not-sky to perch on top of the standing stone.

"How did it go, Æthelred?" Bega asked the bird, and Ivy recognised the lilt of an Irish accent. The seagull tilted its head back and let out a stream of wails that sent her mind back to days at the seaside. Bega chuckled in response.

"The seashell," Ivy said suddenly. It was still in her trouser pocket.

Only you can find your brother. Come through the wall. Seek out Long Meg.

That whisper had had an Irish air, though she hadn't really noticed it at the time.

And the seagulls that had descended upon Taliesin when he tried to steal the glove from her, that had been watching over her ever since she stepped into Underfell—

Ivy pulled the seashell out of her pocket and held it up between her fingers. "You answered my message," she said breathlessly.

Bega smiled wryly. "Calls for help from lost souls tend to find their way to me."

"It's not me who's lost," Ivy protested, clutching the shell tight in her hand. "Well – not exactly. It's my brother, Callum."

"That's not quite what I mean," said Bega. "Listen.

I run a refuge by the sea at St Bees, where people can rest before they continue on their various journeys. Æthelred and his folk have been keeping an eye on you since you came to Underfell, but I thought it was about time we met in person. You've been through so much in the last day or two. I can only imagine how exhausted you must feel."

Until this moment, Ivy had not really stopped to think about how strained her mind was, how much her muscles burned and the soles of her feet ached. But something about these unexpected words of kindness nudged her over an edge she hadn't known she was balancing on, and she felt tears prickling in her eyes.

Still, she shook her head. "No," she said firmly. "I have to find Callum. I don't have time. He doesn't have time. He might—" This was no good; the urge to cry was only getting stronger.

She thought of the map being rent in two, plunging beneath the floodwater. Kit plucking a daisy and sticking it behind his ear. Kit calling Grendel and walking away. The excitement when a path erupted before her and the despair when it didn't. Callum giving chase to the goshawk on the way to school. That last sight of him disappearing into the not-sky.

Ivy shook her head again; tears were brimming in her eyes. "I can't."

To her surprise, Bega laid a hand on her shoulder. She waited until Ivy lifted her eyes to meet her own and then said, "Ivy. You're allowed to give yourself a break."

The weight of Bega's hand, the crinkles around her eyes and the warmth in her smile reminded Ivy painfully of her mum, and that was it. Tears spilled over, flooding down her cheeks, and a few sobs worked their way out of her. Bega passed her a handkerchief to dry her eyes with and she wiped her face roughly. When the flow had mostly ceased and she was merely sniffling, she handed it back.

"All right," Ivy mumbled. "I'll come with you. Thank you."

Bega's smile returned. She pushed her sleeves up her forearms and rolled her shoulders back, turning her body to face the stone.

"I'd teach you this trick if I could, but it's taken me nigh on a thousand years to master. Watch yourself there. It's probably easiest if you hold on to my arm and put your other hand on the stone, flat like this."

Bega had laid the palms of her hands against the rock face. Her knuckles were prominent, her hands callused. For some reason that made Ivy trust her more. She took hold of Bega's arm with one hand as instructed, laying the other against the cool stone.

Bega closed her eyes. The stone began to hum.

Ivy stared at it in wonder for all of one second before the world went dark, and when the light came up again, she was standing on a clifftop.

Bega's Refuge for Wayward Souls

OS Grid Ref: NX 94 14

Ivy found herself in exactly the same position at Bega's side, her palm against rough stone. But waves were crashing against a shore below them and seagulls drifted by overhead. The old grey stone in front of them had been replaced by a burnt-red monolith. Ivy recognised the coastline stretching away from them; they were at the top of St Bees Head, just around the headland from Saltom Pit. She was all the way on the other side of Underfell again.

If they had been in the world above, the wind would have been whipping them off their feet. The stillness of the air here was strange, but the cliff was chaotic with the movement of birds. The piercing cries of guillemots, the squeaks of razorbills, black and white and grey seabirds shifting in their nests, gliding down to the grass, flapping off over the sea. Ivy stood in the centre of it all, eyes wide.

Bega was already turning away along a grassy path

that led inward from the headland. Ivy set off after her, the tufty grass springing back as she lifted her feet. The smell of salt was in the air, even without the wind to carry it.

They passed a flat, smooth piece of driftwood propped up by two posts, carved with the words:

BEGA'S REFUGE FOR WAYWARD SOULS

The path led them to a building tucked into the curve of the cliff. It was a single-storey structure clad in wood that seemed to have been turned a blue-green hue by the sea air. There were tall windows set into the walls at intervals and spreading tendrils of yellow honeysuckle crept up around the frames. The whole thing nestled into the hillside like a fox curled up to sleep.

A number of herring gulls and kittiwakes perched on its flat, grass-covered roof, resting or chattering amongst themselves. They called out in greeting as Bega approached and she waved back at them.

When Bega opened the door, golden light and the warmth of a fire rushed out to meet them. Ivy walked into the glowing building with the feeling of a weight lifting. She hadn't realised it until now, but the steady ambient temperature of Underfell, easy as it was, had been lacking *this*: stepping out into a crisp morning and bracing yourself against the frosty air on your face; rushing to a fireside, stripping off layers of coats and gloves and scarves when you began to sweat; walking to school without a jacket for the first time in the year and shrugging off the spring chill.

Ivy felt a rush of longing for home – not just as she had left it, but as it had been a year ago, before everything that had happened to her, before she had exiled herself indoors.

Bega was removing her weathered leather hiking boots, so Ivy did the same.

"First things first, I think we'd better eat something, don't you?" Bega beckoned for Ivy to follow her down the lamplit hallway.

They stepped into a bright, open room with a wide window overlooking the cliff. Pots and pans hung on a frame suspended from the ceiling; a huge old stove took up most of the far wall, radiating heat. There was a pot the size of a cauldron sitting on the hob and Bega walked up to it and had a sniff.

"We're in luck. French onion soup. One of the other wayward souls is a chef," she said with a grin.

She gestured for Ivy to take a seat at the table, and moments later a bowl of steaming soup was placed in front of her. She picked up a spoon and tucked in. The soup was salty and sweet all at once, and though Ivy had never even considered trying onion soup before, it was in that moment the best thing she had ever tasted. She could practically feel the strength flowing back into her aching limbs, energy seeping back into her tired soul. So when Bega asked if she would like to help her with a task after their meal, she surprised herself by agreeing.

They didn't talk much as they made their way down a narrow path that zigzagged to the shoreline, descending out of the birds' busy nesting zone. The pebbled beach was just quiet enough for them to hear each other.

"I've had another cry for help, from out there." Bega nodded her head in the general direction of the sea. "Thought we might investigate, see if there's anything we can do."

"Out there?" Ivy repeated, looking at the unsettled surface that faded into the amaranthine horizon.

"Are you much of a sailor?" Bega had halted in front of a narrow cave, hands on hips, smiling over her shoulder. Beyond was a small, round boat, like half an acorn.

They carried the coracle to the water together. Bega held it steady, waist-deep in the sea, completely unfazed by the waves that rolled past her, soaking her jeans.

"Jump in!" she instructed. Ivy took hold of the edge of the flimsy-looking craft and hauled herself over, landing ungracefully on her bum. Bega hopped lightly in after her and helped pull her up onto the seat.

"Is this thing big enough for two?" Ivy asked uncertainly.

"She's never failed me yet." Bega patted the side of the craft. She began to paddle them forwards with the single long oar.

Bega's strong strokes took them far from the shore in a matter of minutes. For Ivy this was another realm entirely:

far off the map, where there were no paths at all, only winds and currents. She felt herself untethered again, like when she had flown on Peregrine's back. But it was hard for anxiety to sink in in the presence of someone like Bega, who seemed so capable and sure of herself.

To Ivy's delight, she found that it was easy to see down into the depths of the sea here, and the water was teeming with life. Moon jellyfish propelled themselves beneath their vessel; rays drifted by like spaceships; dolphins leapt out of the surf just metres away.

A pod of seals was turning somersaults in the waves, and these seemed to catch Bega's eye. One of their dog-like, guileless faces popped out of the water right beside them, all smiling whiskers, and seemed to beckon them in with a jerk of its head as it rolled back under the surface. Bega's powerful strokes paused for the briefest moment as she lingered over the place where the seal had vanished, but then she narrowed her eyes and pushed them onwards, and Ivy was soon able to pick out what she thought Bega was focusing on: a silver buoy bobbing in the waves.

Bega gestured to it. "Can you grab that for me?"

Ivy looked out at the water with trepidation, but she nodded. She reached over the side of the coracle as far as she could to grab the buoy. Gripping onto a loop of frayed rope tied through a ring, she hauled it into the boat. The buoy itself was light, but the rope disappeared down into the fathomless sea, and there was something heavy at the other end.

"What is this?" Ivy asked.

"This is our cry for help," Bega replied with a waggle of her eyebrows. She began to tow in the rope, one hand over the other. Ivy shuffled out of the way as Bega threw her weight backwards, pulling the object out of the water with her.

It was a lobster pot. Ivy had seen them piled on the docks when they visited the coast, half a wooden cylinder covered with mesh, wound round with coarse ropes. A single creature huddled at the back of the trap, and its long whiskers and spindly legs were trembling with fear.

"Lobster," Bega informed her. "Or so it would appear."

"So it needs our help to get out of the trap?" Ivy guessed.

"In a way. This is the creature whose cry for help I heard – that much I'm sure of. But this is no ordinary trap." Ivy, who was not particularly knowledgeable when it came to lobster pots, could not have said what was ordinary or extraordinary about it. "This is a spellwork," Bega concluded.

Ivy's breath caught as she remembered Long Meg's gravelly voice: *There's only one fairy whose spellworks take the form of songs.* "What is a spellwork, exactly?" she asked. "I don't think I understand how magic works at all."

"A spellwork is one of the three elements needed for magic here," Bega explained. "It's the physical form that the spell takes. To make a spell, you have to craft something. In this case, a lobster pot." She lifted the trap, which was resting on her knees. "But there are two other elements. You must have an intention, of course. For example, 'I want to cook a good meal for my friend, the best she's ever eaten.' That's an intention."

"Or, 'I want to turn a boy into a kestrel,'" Ivy supplied.

Bega nodded. "Right."

Ivy thought carefully for a moment. "Taliesin was singing when he transformed Callum," she said. "Long Meg said that was a spellwork."

Bega was looking over the lobster inside the pot, examining it for injuries. "Yes, Taliesin's spellworks are well known," she said. "They say he's the only fairy whose spellworks don't take a lasting physical form. That makes him very powerful indeed."

Ivy devoured this information, though it made her uneasy. "So what's the third element?" she pushed.

"The catalyst," Bega answered. "An emotion. It has to be strong. You see, you can't go around making magic unless you really want it. Otherwise all the fairies would be whipping up meringues out of thin air whenever they felt peckish. Magic is meaningful, and it has to be fed by feeling. Let's take this as an example." She gestured to the lobster pot in her lap again. "I don't know the story here, but I can guess along the lines of it. Let's say a fisher has been stealing from their neighbour's lobster pots. That neighbour gets it into their head to teach the thief a lesson – that's their *intention*. They use their anger and frustration as the *catalyst* for the magic, they *craft* the lobster pot themselves to work the magic in. Then the thief comes along and reels in the pot, and what do you know – the spell turns them into a lobster."

Ivy gaped at the frightened creature in the pot. "Is that what's happened here?"

"I don't think so." Bega looked closely at the lobster. "I think someone has set off this trap by accident."

Ivy stared at the pot, worrying for its inhabitant, wondering about their true form, and trying to apply this new understanding to Callum. "Before he changed, Callum gave me a stone," she told Bega. "A fairy bead. Is that a kind of spellwork?"

"Yes. A very old kind."

Ivy's mind raced over everything Taliesin had hinted or threatened in their encounters. "Taliesin said they would only work on a particular person – no one else," she said. "Is that true?"

Bega pondered this. "It's not entirely a lie," she said slowly. "Spellworks are certainly most effective on the person they're intended for, but that doesn't mean others are immune to them. Innocent bystanders can become bound up in magic in all sorts of ways. The most powerful fairies don't even need to use their own feelings as a catalyst; they can draw on other people's."

Then there were two spells here: the bead, and Callum's transformation. That brought Ivy to the most important question of all. "So how can you undo a spell?"

The lobster shuffled in its pot, catching a leg in the knotted rope. "Let's see what we can do here first," Bega said. "I'll hold the pot, and you untangle the poor creature. Then we'll take it out."

"All right."

Bega pointed out a couple of knots on the pot that Ivy needed to untie, and she worked her fingers around the tough rope until a panel fell open and she was able to reach inside.

Ivy had never seen a lobster up close before, but she steeled herself and moved her arm slowly into the pot. The lobster didn't lunge at her or try to pinch her with its claws; it just sat there, looking nervous. She reached for the rope knotted around it and gradually pushed it down off the limb.

The creature looked like it wanted to move again but wasn't quite sure. Ivy offered her flat palm for it to scuttle onto, but it didn't seem to get the message. So she braced herself, wrapped her hand around its cold, slippery body and drew it out. Its legs pinwheeled as she pulled it free.

The moment the little form was free of the lobster pot, the coracle tipped and Ivy lost her grip as hard shell became slippery skin. She grabbed onto the side of the boat as the lobster exploded into an unfathomably huge creature that plunged straight over the side into the water, sending up a spray that soaked them both. The coracle rocked violently for a few moments before it settled back into the steady rhythm of the waves.

"What was *that*?" asked Ivy, breathless.

Bega was staring into the water. Suddenly she pointed. "There!"

Ivy scrambled backwards in fright. There were two black fins slicing through the waves around the coracle. When she dared to look over the edge, she saw that they were attached to an animal bigger than anything she had seen before; it could have been ten metres long. It had a wide grey head with huge gills that fanned out as it swam, fins like great wings in the water, and a tail that propelled the colossal body forwards by sweeping from side to side.

Then it opened its mouth wide and Ivy almost fell back over the seat. Its gaping mouth hung twice as low as the rest of its body, and the interior looked as though it were propped up by bone-white ribs.

"*That's* the lobster?" Ivy said in disbelief when she finally found her voice.

Bega laughed with delight. "Our lobster is a basking shark!" Ivy's expression of open-mouthed wonder was reflected on Bega's face.

The basking shark did another lap around the coracle, then curved away from them and went on its way. They watched it go in silence.

"But how did that happen?" Ivy asked. "Do you think it just… got tangled in the rope, or touched the lobster pot, and was trapped by the spell?"

"That's what I suspect," said Bega. She began to wind up the rope, looping it expertly over her palm and elbow.

"So to undo the spell all we had to do was take away the spellwork?"

"In this case, yes," Bega agreed, not looking at her. "When the spellwork is a physical object, it's fairly straightforward to unmake."

Ivy's heart sank as she realised what that meant for Callum. "But Taliesin's spellworks aren't physical," she said, dismayed. "As soon as they're finished, they're gone."

Bega didn't respond; she took up the oar again and drove it into the water, turning the coracle towards home.

Ivy felt her hopes sinking into the depths of the sea. "Can you even unmake a spell like that?" she asked.

Bega paused with her hands on the oar, sighed, then held it out to Ivy. "Mind if you paddle? Storytelling and navigation don't really go hand in hand."

Intrigued, Ivy took the oar from her and began to row. She discovered immediately that the round boat was a nightmare to steer: it spun in one direction, then the other, barely making any progress. She had to move quickly from one side to the next and push with all her strength to make any headway at all.

Bega sat back on her bench.

"Up above, a long time ago, I grew up with a fairy father and a human mother. When my father arranged a marriage for me, I fled Ireland in this coracle. I could barely keep my head above water, so to speak, overcome with anger at my father, grief for leaving behind my family and my home. Relief and excitement too, in smaller measures. Somewhere along the way, I felt magic stirring."

"Your father turned you into a seal," Ivy put in.

"Is that what they say?" A wry smile twisted Bega's mouth as she stared down at the water. "It is true that I became a seal. I was desperate to escape and I was in emotional turmoil. Being only half-fairy, I don't often perform magic, and when I do, it is a long, slow process. I was out on the sea for many days."

Ivy stopped what she was doing; the oar hovered above the water. "*You* made the spell?"

Bega leaned forwards and clasped her hands, elbows resting on her knees. "By accident," she said. "I swam to St Bees underwater, and for three years I lived off the coast among the seals, barely coming ashore at all."

"But what was your spellwork?" Ivy asked.

Bega shook her head. "I'm honestly not sure," she said. "It might have been the stories I made up for the gulls that flew with me, or songs I sang as I fished. I don't even remember what I was doing when I slipped over the side of the coracle and plopped into the sea."

Ivy realised the boat had been spinning in slow circles and returned to her task, though she was brimming with questions.

"If there is no spellwork to remove, there are still two more elements that can be unravelled in order to unmake a spell. But it's far more difficult, and not just anyone can do it," Bega went on. "In my years as a seal I swam much deeper than the Irish Sea, and when at last

I stepped ashore as a woman again, it was in Underfell. My *intention* was the same: I still wanted to escape. But the feelings that had formed the *catalyst* had changed. I had settled; I had let go of my anger and grief. Once the catalyst was gone, the spell fell apart."

Bega spread her hands as if to say, *and here I am*. She was not looking at Ivy any more, though. Her eyes were fixed on the sea beyond.

They were approaching the shore at last. Ivy brought the oar into the boat, and the coracle swayed steadily.

Bega's last remark had set the cogs in her mind turning, generating a flutter of hope. "If it's all about feelings," she asked, "if I want it enough, can I break the spell myself?"

Bega was watching her patiently, her expression betraying nothing. "It's not as simple as that," she replied. "The counter-spellwork would have to come from the same person whose feeling created the spell in the first place. It must be an answer to the catalyst, its opposite, something with the power to undo it."

Ivy felt herself deflate. "So even when I finally find Callum, I'll have to find Taliesin again. I can't do it on my own."

"I expect he'll come to you, when the moment is right," Bega answered. "But I don't think it will be as simple as just bringing the two of them together. I think you're missing important pieces of the puzzle."

Then she hopped out of the boat, splashing into the waves. Ivy followed suit, enjoying the sensation of the cool water seeping into her trousers. They lifted the coracle together and returned her to the cave, then made their way back up to the refuge.

Once they were back inside, Bega showed Ivy to a room where she could stay for the night. There was a single bed tucked into an alcove in the wall, and a desk beneath the window which overlooked the sea. Dread pooled in Ivy's stomach as she looked at it.

"I've already wasted too much time." She stepped away from the door, then felt immediately embarrassed. "Sorry, not wasted, I just mean – Callum doesn't have much time, and I need to get back to looking for him."

"You won't get far in the dark." Bega gestured to the window, where violet night was already beginning to fall. "I won't stop you, Ivy. But I strongly recommend a good night's sleep and a hearty breakfast. The hardest problems are often solved that way."

Ivy felt herself resisting, but she forced herself to see the truth in Bega's words.

"Maybe tomorrow I could call on Peregrine again," she said in a small voice as the idea struck her.

Bega pursed her lips. "I must advise caution," she replied gently. "Peregrine is only loyal to one man. Once may be a gift – twice, a debt. You don't want to owe any creature of Underfell a favour."

Her heart sinking, Ivy walked inside and set down her pack, almost too afraid to ask the question that had been ringing in her mind since she'd arrived. Bega lingered in the doorway as though she could sense the words unasked.

"Do you... do you have a map I could borrow?" Ivy said at last. "I lost mine, and... I take really good care of them usually, it was because of a flood and a ghost and... I would bring it back to you, I promise, I just..."

She trailed off. Bega's sad smile was answer enough. "I'm sorry, Ivy. There aren't any maps of Underfell."

Ivy dropped her gaze. The idea of continuing to fumble her way around this strange place without any sort of guide, under this unfamiliar sky, was almost too much to bear. She'd pinned all her hopes on Bega having something. Anything.

Bega had a thoughtful look on her face as she regarded Ivy. "How long have you lived in Cumbria?" she asked.

Ivy shrugged. "Thirteen years. I was born here. There."

"A whole life of rambling and mountain climbing," said Bega. "I wouldn't think you'd need to read a map at all, Ivy. I'd think you could draw one in your mind."

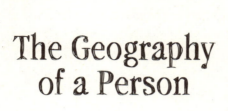

The Geography of a Person

OS Grid Ref: NY 21 13

Ivy slept until her body told her to wake up. When she finally opened her eyes her limbs were heavy, as though she'd given them permission to hibernate. She lay in bed for a long time, letting awareness seep gradually back into her body and mind.

Callum.

She jumped out of bed. The moment her feet hit the floor, the bone-tiredness vanished. It could have been the deep sleep, or the warming winter stew they'd eaten the night before, or the long soak she'd had in the bath afterwards. She felt thoroughly refreshed.

Today she must set out on her own, without the map, to bring Callum home. She had the glove; that was something. And a plan was taking shape in her mind.

After he had been transformed, after he'd been chased away from the wall by Taliesin's hawfinches, maybe Callum had flown somewhere he knew she would come looking for him. Maybe he had settled down to wait for her there. It was a slim but tantalising hope.

She would go to the places he loved, one by one, until she found where he was waiting for her. Castlerigg Stone Circle, where Iona always took them for a picnic on the summer solstice. The ruins of Pendragon Castle, built by King Arthur's dad, according to legend anyway.

Then it struck her. There was one place Callum talked about more than any other.

The Bowder Stone.

In her memory of the map, which seemed to fade every time she tried to grasp at it, the Bowder Stone had been almost directly east of where she stood now. That would mean heading inland from the coast and into the fells, passing through Ennerdale and maybe Buttermere…

If only she could check her map.

When Ivy entered the kitchen that morning Bega was at the counter already, slicing a loaf of freshly baked bread that released a sheet of steam as the knife cut into it. Ivy gratefully piled her plate with it, slathering the slices in butter that turned to liquid almost as soon as it touched the doughy surface.

"You look like you're ready to set off," Bega said as they sat down opposite each other at the table.

Ivy swallowed the mouthful she had been chewing. "I feel much better today. I can't keep Callum waiting any longer."

Bega nodded in understanding. "It was very brave of you to come to Underfell, Ivy."

Ivy's automatic response was to roll her eyes, but then she felt immediately embarrassed and mumbled, "Sorry." Bega was still looking at her politely. She cleared her throat and said, "I'm not brave. I'm his sister. I'm supposed to look after him… but it's the other way around. Since what happened a year ago… He's only nine, but he's the one who's been looking after me."

To her shame, she felt hot tears fill her eyes again. She knew she should be quiet, but the words kept coming. "Afraid of coming off the path. Afraid of the sky and the mountains. I'm a pathetic big sister. I couldn't even go through the wall to get him when he was calling for me."

The tears spilled over and leaked down her cheeks; she wiped them away, staring down at her plate as though it might make her invisible.

"You've come to a place where the paths don't play by your rules," Bega said softly. "Where sometimes they don't appear at all. Where there's a different sky altogether. I'd say that's one of the bravest things you can do for someone you love."

"For all the good it's done him," Ivy said bitterly.

Bega was silent for another moment. "I can't make you see what's in front of you," she said. "I can only tell you it's there."

Ivy sniffed and wiped away the tears again, determined that these would be the last ones that fell. She made herself meet Bega's eyes. "Thank you for bringing me here," she said. "Giving me a chance to rest. I did need it.

I just hope…" She trailed off.

"Callum will be fine," Bega said firmly. "How could he not be, with you looking out for him?"

Ivy's thoughts strayed to Kit, who had never given up on Billy, all this time.

"Can I ask you something?" She was not quite sure how to word it. "If it's lost souls that you want to help, why didn't – how come you never brought Kit here?"

To Ivy's surprise Bega dropped her gaze, her cheeks flushing faintly red. "I'm ashamed to say he slipped my notice," she admitted. "Kit is the very definition of a wayward soul. He never actually gave a cry for help… When Æthelred reported that you'd found a human boy who had been wandering for a hundred years, I was astonished, and dismayed to have missed him. After all, this is exactly the sort of thing the Refuge exists for."

Ivy didn't know what to say to that. Every time she heard or thought the words *a hundred years* she flinched inwardly, trying not to imagine Kit alone and confused for all that time. But Kit hadn't even known he was lost to ask for help. That was the most painful thing of all.

"You'll be pleased to know that Æthelred returned again this morning," Bega went on. "His folk have been keeping an eye on Kit and Grendel since you parted ways. He has found the court of King Eveling."

"Oh, good," Ivy said, though her eyes were filling with tears again and this time she wasn't even sure why. Relief and sadness mingled in the pit of her stomach. Would Kit get his wish? Find Billy and get him home, and never think of her again? That sent an ache into her wrists and palms and she rubbed them, trying to soothe herself.

"Does that hurt?" Bega nodded to the silver impression of a hand curled around her forearm.

"It doesn't bother me at all," Ivy said, grateful to be distracted. "It makes me feel kind of – safe, actually. I suppose Æthelred told you about the tup fair? Naveen said it meant I was protected, because the Spectre King couldn't drain the colour from me."

But then she saw that pale grey hand tearing through the map again, and her mouth went dry. She took a sip of her orange juice and asked, "Why do you think he's been following me? Is it because I'm human? Or because of something Callum did?"

Bega finished her bread and dusted crumbs from her fingers. "I wish I could tell you," she said. "Sometimes there is no way to outrun the thing that pursues us; all we can do is to turn around and face it head on."

Ivy didn't quite know what to say to that. Finding Callum was her first and only priority.

When their meal was finished, Ivy went to her room and packed up her bag, laced up her hiking boots, and re-plaited her hair.

Bega was waiting by the door. They stepped out into the hazy violet day together.

"There's Dent." Bega pointed out the nearest low fell. "Ennerdale isn't far beyond it. You'll find your way from there."

Ivy nodded, trying to project a confidence she didn't feel. For a fleeting moment she wasn't sure quite what to do, then she threw her arms around Bega and hugged her tightly. She felt a rush of longing for her mum's crushing hugs that smelled of clay and lavender, and at the same time gratitude for Bega, who hugged her back with warmth, then patted her on the shoulder and let her go.

Ivy set one foot in front of the other and started to walk.

At first, with the sea behind her and Dent ahead, it was easy enough to keep her mind off the fact that there was no path. Before the sea disappeared behind the hills, Ivy took out her compass and picked the outline of a fell directly east of where she stood. Then she marched towards that, the compass in her hand.

She did not know which paths should be underfoot, so none revealed themselves to her. But she tried to keep her thoughts away from that by turning over everything Bega had said. She wondered about Kit, imagining him and Grendel being welcomed into King Eveling's court, his wish being granted, his reunion with Billy.

Kit's absence was a deep ache: the way he'd leave a trail of shredded reeds and beheaded stems of bog cotton in his wake, dart off the path in search of a harvest mouse he'd seen in the grass, suddenly race

Grendel to the end of the field. She had been so stupid to take him for granted, to keep putting herself first. She had driven him away.

Eventually she came to the familiar shores of Ennerdale and began to trace her way along the lakeside. If she passed through the forest at the other end she could climb High Stile to get a better view; perhaps that would jog her memory.

But by the time she reached the summit, her heart was hammering. There was a feeling blooming in the pit of her stomach, climbing up into her chest and spreading out through her limbs: *you don't know where you're going*. How clearly did she actually remember that visit to the Bowder Stone with Iona and Callum? All she recalled was a river, and Callum silent with wonder as he climbed the stone. For all she knew, the Bowder Stone was on the other side of Underfell, and by the time she finally found Callum, it would be too late.

Her vision narrowed in on the blank ground ahead of her. The sounds of birdsong and a distant waterfall grew dim and faint.

It took her a long time – too long – to hear the cry of a bird of prey.

"Callum!" she shouted, looking wildly about. It was like a bubble had burst and she could see and hear the world around her in sharp focus again. She saw the outline of a soaring bird in the not-sky above, too distant for her to identify.

But it must be him, she told herself. *It must be.*

215

"CALLUM!" she called again, louder than she knew she was capable of. She went careening along the fellside in the bird's wake, trying to follow its path through the sky from way below, running to keep up with its pace.

The bird soared higher into the sky, and she ran until she began to stumble, paying no heed to her surroundings. She slowed to a fast walk, caught her breath, waited until her legs felt less like jelly and more like legs, and started running again.

The glove. She had the glove; she could summon him to her. The bird was already becoming a distant speck when Ivy stopped dead. She yanked the straps off her shoulders and tore through the bag until the glove was in her hand, and she pulled it onto her fist and raised her arm—

But the bird was gone.

Ivy called his name anyway, kept her fist raised, scanning the not-sky, until finally she was forced to accept that the bird was nowhere in sight. That, if she really thought about it, the cry she'd heard hadn't sounded much like a kestrel's at all.

She kept walking, telling herself that soon she would see a landmark she recognised and be able to get back on track. But her gaze fell to the ground beneath her, and there was nothing but grass and flowers under her boots, stretching out in every direction. No guide, no marker. The grey fog began to creep in at the edges of her vision, and she closed her eyes tight against it and stopped walking.

She was lost, and she was very far from home. Iona would not come striding in to save her this time. Callum was gone and she didn't know how to get him back. She had failed.

As she pressed her hands to her face and her breathing quickened, images sprang up unbidden behind her eyes. Their grey slate house. Beckfoot. The outline of the fells from her bedroom window. In her mind she pictured her creased old map and traced the pencilled routes to school, to the village shop, to the library. She remembered every walk – Iona leading the way, she and Callum tripping along in her wake, and then, as she got older, striding out in front herself with the map tucked in her pocket.

She would stop and read it and take a bearing, but always to check what she already knew. Iona would point out the silhouettes of the fells in the distance and get her to identify them. Ivy knew the curves the rivers took, the sheep paths, the humpback bridges. Her mind had shaped itself around the countryside.

She lowered her hands and opened her eyes.

She was on a grassy plateau between high grey crags. Had she been at home, strong winds would have been whistling through them, making her ears ache. To a lost traveller this place might seem forbidding and harsh, a fortress of stone. But Ivy just looked and looked, letting the sight of it wash over her with a rush of relief so strong she had to gulp down a sob.

She knew where she was.

She walked across the plateau to the east. When she looked down into the valley she knew at once what she would find there.

Even from where Ivy stood, high on the ridge, she felt the trembling of the earth. Cobbles began to pop out of the ground like molehills. Clouds of dust rose into the air, and rabbits and deer fled from the commotion.

Finally everything stilled, and there it was: the old Roman road that had once wound through the pass, long since buried beneath tarmac in the world above.

She could follow this road down to a valley, and there, she knew, she would find the Bowder Stone.

Once Ivy's feet hit the Roman road, every step she took on the uneven cobbles sent a wave of gratitude through her body. Her boots devoured the ground in long strides that brought her to the foot of the valley in no time at all.

She raised her head and scanned the surrounding fells slowly, cataloguing every feature of the landscape and recalling its counterpart up above. She didn't shrink from the sky or not-sky or whatever it was – the shades of violet were extraordinary, and the air was fresh and filled with birdsong.

Bega was right. She didn't need to read a map: she could read the landscape.

She made her way to the bank of a wide, steady river and began to follow it upstream. She wasn't on the Roman road any more, but she no longer needed a path to guide her steps. She knew she was heading in the right direction.

Ivy had thought that she might keel over with relief and excitement when she found it, but when she stepped into the shadow of the great boulder she had been seeking, she was filled was a steady sort of calm. She felt grounded, rooted, for the first time in a long time.

The Bowder Stone was Callum's favourite place in Cumbria. In a lush green valley, half-hidden amongst trees, rose a colossal stone that looked as though it had been knocked from a mountaintop by a giant and then frozen in motion by a spell. It had the peculiar quality of looking utterly solid, and at the same time, as if a breath of wind might just send it rolling on its way. The Victorians had called it the biggest boulder known to man and built a staircase to the top.

Ivy let her eyes fall closed.

It didn't matter if Callum wasn't here; she would work down the list of places that he might be waiting for her, and she knew now that she could find her way. Time may not be on her side, but at the rate she could travel around Underfell, she had a chance.

At the cry of a kestrel her eyes snapped open.

There was a bird of prey turning slow circles in the sky above the Bowder Stone, with a pale cream underbelly and black tips to its tail feathers. It angled its small, curved beak towards her and called again. Even with the distance between them, she knew at once. Her heart sang with the certainty of it.

Callum.

Listen to the Birds

OS Grid Ref: NY 25 16

Ivy threw down her bag, tore the glove from within and sprinted to the steps, using two hands on the railings to pull herself as fast as she could to the Bowder Stone's peak.

At the top of the rock she stuffed her hand into the glove, held her arm up high and called, "Callum!"

He turned and dove towards her, making a graceful beeline for her arm. Even with his wings out wide he was so small, so swift! *What must it have been like to borrow the body of a kestrel?* Ivy wondered, but in the next moment, her mind went blank with fear.

Another bird had appeared from nowhere, slicing across her line of sight, making directly for Callum. It was a mammoth creature, so much bigger than the little falcon that was her brother, a blur of black and white that streaked across the sky towards him.

The osprey from the falconer's tower.

Callum noticed it in the same moment she did. He let out a squeak, changing course rapidly to narrowly avoid its outstretched claws. Then they were tussling in the air, a ball of feathers and beating wings as kestrel-Callum tried to elude the osprey's grasp.

"NESSA!"

Ivy knew that voice.

The falconer emerged, breathless, into the clearing below the stone. Her amber eyes were fixed on the great bird of prey above them, tracing its path across the sky, and she barely spared a glance for Ivy before she yelled, "Throw me the glove!"

Ivy didn't hesitate. She slipped her hand free and tossed the heavy leather glove into the clearing, where the falconer deftly caught it. She put it on and punched a fist into the air.

"NESSA!" The emblem on the glove began to crackle and glow.

Just like that, the osprey removed itself from the fray, beating its great wings to haul itself back, and gracefully descended to the ground. The falconer's arm sank under the weight of the enormous creature as it came to rest.

But Callum was coming too, and Ivy could only watch in wonder as he soared down to the stone and alighted on the railing, chirping animatedly. All at once, Ivy was certain that Callum was still Callum in there. Tears of relief and joy sprang to her eyes and began flowing down her cheeks unchecked. She held out her arm and he hopped onto it without hesitation, his sharp little claws digging in.

His feathers were ruffled by the scuffle in the air, but otherwise he looked healthy and well. Ivy reached out a hand and gently brushed the feathers on his chest. Most of his body was the colour of honey flecked with arrowheads of dark brown, though his head and tail were grey, his legs and beak bright yellow.

"Thank you for waiting for me," she murmured. "I'm sorry I took so long."

Kestrel-Callum just kept chirruping away, and she didn't think she was imagining the happiness in his eyes.

Slowly Ivy descended the staircase, hoping to somehow delay the inevitable. The falconer was standing in the clearing with a wide stance, the huge bird supported on her outstretched arm, regarding Ivy with a sharp look. The bottom dropped out of Ivy's stomach as she approached, remembering vividly the falconer's yells as she had fled with the stolen glove; the subsequent night of fear and flight was still fresh in her memory.

"You can calm down. I haven't been following *you*," the falconer said. Ivy's confusion must have shown on her face because the woman added, "I've been following *her*." She lifted her weightbearing arm slightly to indicate the osprey.

Ivy was impressed she could move it at all under the weight of the giant raptor. The falconer was a little shorter than Ivy, but her arms were ropey with muscle.

Ivy took a deep breath. "I'm sorry for stealing from you," she said in a rush. "I know it was the wrong thing to do."

To Ivy's surprise, the woman just shook her head, dismissing her words. "I see why you took it." She nodded to the kestrel perched on Ivy's sleeve. "Friend of yours?"

"He's my brother," Ivy replied, and Callum chirped as if to support her.

"I see," said the falconer. "The thing is, I would have lent it to you if you'd asked." She grinned. "I'm Yun." She held out her free hand and Ivy took it in hers, heat rising to her cheeks as they shook.

"I'm Ivy. Sorry," she squeaked again. "I... It's not an excuse, but I was warned to keep away from you."

Yun's heavy brow furrowed. The osprey shifted its weight and she winced. "Who would have told you a thing like that?"

At the sound of wingbeats, they both looked up. Ivy had to hold back a groan as she watched Taliesin land lightly on his feet beside them, rustle his colourful wings as if to shake off the dust and then tuck them neatly behind his back.

"That may have been me," he said with false sheepishness. "I see you've reclaimed your glove, Falconer." He turned his gaze on Ivy, sharp eyes seeking out the kestrel on her arm. "And this must be Callum, at last."

Ivy drew her brother in close to her body to shield him. "What took you so long?" she said sarcastically. Taliesin scowled. Callum's round black eyes darted over the fairy and away again, but he made no sound. Ivy wondered if he knew the face of the man who had transformed him.

Yun's face was creased with barely concealed disdain as she regarded Taliesin. "I'm surprised to see you here alone," she said. "I thought the two of you were joined at the hip."

"That's none of your concern." Taliesin's voice was colder than Ivy had ever heard it.

"Why are you pestering the girl?" the falconer pressed. "Warned her away from me because you thought I might help, is that it? She steal something from you too?"

"I would have given the glove back," Ivy grumbled.

Taliesin ran a critical eye over Yun from head to foot, arms folded across his chest. There was clearly no love lost between these two. "Yes, she did. Her brother stole a spellwork of mine, and she helped him conceal it and lied about it. I've come to retrieve it."

"For the last time, we don't have the bead!" Ivy cried in exasperation. "I've told you we don't."

"Not a song, then?" Yun asked with sudden interest, ignoring Ivy. "They couldn't have stolen it if you'd sung the spell."

"I know." Taliesin's mouth was set in a thin line. "It was a very old spellwork."

Yun raised her eyebrows.

Ivy decided it was time to clear this up once and for all. She cleared her throat. "Taliesin, I haven't got the fairy bead. Neither has Callum. I don't know how he came by it, but he did give it to me, and I kept it from you. But then I lost it. I truly don't have it any more.

I give you whatever magical permission you need to search us both so you can see that I'm telling the truth."

Trepidation seized hold of her chest as she said it, but then the strangest thing happened: as Taliesin listened to her, the hard lines around his eyes and mouth softened. He looked young again, open and kind the way he had been pictured on the banner at Saltom town hall. He looked hopeful. She felt her anxiety recede.

"All right." He rolled back his shoulders and closed his eyes. Beside Ivy, Yun sighed and threw up her arm, sending Nessa into the not-sky.

There was a sound in the air like the buzzing of bees, melodious and resonant. It was Taliesin – he was humming, and the sound was growing louder, and then the hum became words that Ivy didn't understand. The otherworldly music washed over her, and she felt a peculiar sensation – a kind of stirring, sweeping up from her toes to her forehead, rustling her clothes like a breeze.

In a moment it was gone. The song had stopped, and Taliesin was staring at her. She felt uncomfortably as though she had disappointed him.

"It's gone." He blinked at her as though he didn't even know who she was. Then he turned and began to walk towards the stone.

"Wait," Ivy said numbly, gathering her thoughts, and ran after him. "Wait! Taliesin!"

He was halfway up the steps already, his head down, not looking at any of them. Callum muttered and adjusted his weight on her arm as she sprang up the steps.

"You have to help us! You have to turn Callum back. You need to break the spell!"

At the top of the stone her words finally seemed to sink in, and Taliesin turned slowly towards her.

"I can't," he said softly.

Then he threw out his wings and launched himself upwards with such force that she was almost swept down the steps in the downdraft.

"WAIT!" Ivy called after him, feeling as though all of her hard-won optimism was being blown away. "PLEASE!" Her voice broke, but he didn't look back. She watched her last hope fly off into the purple haze.

Ivy growled her frustration and tossed a pebble uselessly after him; he was already almost out of sight. Distantly she heard Yun chuckle at her efforts, and she descended the steps feeling as though she had been cut adrift once more. She had found Callum, but he was a bird, and the one person who could help her just… wouldn't.

Yun seemed to swim into focus before her, and an idea struck Ivy. "Can you help us?" she asked desperately. "Have you seen this happen before? Do you know how we can turn him back?"

"I'm sorry," Yun said gently, and Ivy felt her heart sink further. "I don't know much about that sort of thing. I don't have any magic – only the glove, and that was a gift."

Yun must have read the gloom written on her face because she went on. "Listen, I won't give you any trouble about the glove. I know what he's like, and your heart was in the right place, I think. Important thing is, I've got it back now. They're not all necessarily *trained*, you see."

This was followed by a pointed glare at Nessa, wheeling high over their heads. "They're rescues. Not able to fend for themselves for long; that's why I had to chase her night and day. She can't hunt for herself – she may look scary, but your brother would've got away in the end. She's new to my place. The others are getting the hang of it, they come back without the glove all right, but she still needs a bit of enchantment. Takes them a while to trust me."

She had Ivy's attention now, even through the fog of disappointment and worry. "Is that what you were doing with the buzzard?" she asked. "Looking after it?"

Yun nodded. "Saw that, did you? Yeah, I keep an eye on the populations. If I see a wild bird I tend to call 'em in to check how they're faring."

"That's amazing." Ivy suddenly wished deeply that she had not let Taliesin worry her and had just knocked on that tower door. How differently the last few days might have gone.

Yun was looking around now, rubbing her hands over her ears, eyes squinting. "How can you handle all this noise?" she asked. "You must have a blinding headache!"

Ivy paused to listen, tuning in to the torrent of

birdsong that had accompanied her every step through Underfell. "The birds?" she questioned. "Is that not normal here?"

"Normal!" Yun barked a laugh. "Well, they're a bit chatty, but this – I don't know how you manage with them shouting at you like this all day!"

"Shouting?" Ivy laughed, but then she stopped, sensing another layer to her meaning. "Wait, do you mean you can understand what they're saying?"

"Oh, yeah," Yun replied, then frowned at her. "Can you not?"

Despite everything, Ivy's mouth spread into a bemused smile. "No, I can't understand birds!"

"Yes, you can," Yun said in an unimpressed tone that made Ivy stand up straighter. "You haven't heard anything odd? Voices talking when there's no one around? You would have noticed it when you weren't thinking too hard."

Ivy felt her jaw slacken as she thought back over the past few days, to the disembodied voices that had woken her more than once.

"I did…" she murmured.

Yun laughed. "You're used to tuning out birdsong. Most people are. But have you ever actually *tried* to understand it? Focus. Listen…"

Ivy frowned, and as she did so, she felt like she was letting her ears relax, letting her mind loosen just a little bit.

And then she heard it.

heartwood heartwood heartwood
Heartwood Heartwood
HEARTWOOD
HEARTWOOD
HEARTWOOD

"Heartwood?" Ivy tested it out. It had a ring of familiarity, partially blurred by strangeness. "Is that what you're hearing, Yun?"

The falconer's lips quirked in a smile. "Yes."

"Why would they be telling me that?" Ivy wondered aloud, even as her ears continued to ring with the sound of it: pigeons and blue tits and herons and kingfishers, a hundred different voices, all of them calling to her: *Heartwood.*

"Sounds like a place," Yun offered. "You don't know it?"

Ivy looked down at the kestrel on her arm watching her hopefully, and around at the trees trembling with birds. "I know a place," she said. "It's just, I thought that was only *my* name for it. There's a wood in the shape of a heart. You can see it from the motorway…"

"I have no idea what a motorway is, but it seems like you maybe want to go there," said Yun. "I'm not sure they'll shut up until you do."

Ivy closed her eyes, picturing that cluster of trees she always looked out for when they travelled out of the county and back, that little insignificant woodland that had always told her she was home again.

Heartwood.

A Gift for a Wish

OS Grid Ref: NY 48 11

Ivy moved through the landscape in her mind: down the valley along the riverbank, over the fells towards Ambleside, between the tarns and crags at the foot of Haweswater. There, she knew, she would find the beginning of the old corpse road which would lead her most of the way to the Heartwood.

She apologised to Yun one last time before they went their separate ways, but all the falconer said was, "Don't do it again." Ivy wasn't sure she'd balanced the scales of good deeds to bad, but at least she had been able to return the glove.

She didn't know what lay in wait for her at the Heartwood, but she had decided to trust the birds. Perhaps some had been spying on her in Underfell, but she had always loved and respected them back home. She held on to a quiet belief that most of them were trying to help her and Callum, whatever their reasons may be.

When Ivy started to walk, no path emerged from

the ground ahead of her. This wasn't surprising in itself, since she was not picturing a specific path, only following her instincts. But she felt a subtle rumble in the earth with each step she took that perplexed her until finally she had the bright idea to check behind her.

What she found made her stop in her tracks.

Where she stepped, she was leaving a path in her wake. It was little more than packed earth and flattened grass, but it was as clear as any of the paths she'd followed before.

She was carving her own trail through Underfell.

Callum sometimes rested on her shoulder or her arm as they travelled, but most of the time he soared a few metres above her, speeding ahead and then doubling back, his wings sharp and graceful. It was mesmerising to be so close to a kestrel when she had only ever seen them from a distance before, or through the lenses of her binoculars. But then some time would pass when she couldn't see or hear him at all. After a little while he'd come soaring back again, but those episodes still made her uneasy.

Callum generally seemed to be in high spirits, although Ivy couldn't understand his chirps – perhaps he hadn't learned the birds' tricks for communicating in Underfell.

The flocks that urged them onwards were as noisy as ever, but she could only pick out what they were saying if she focused. *Heartwood, Heartwood.*

They came to the fells around Haweswater, which she

recognised now that the valley was filled with water as it was in the Cumbria she knew. She passed into a bright oak woodland where the forest floor was carpeted with bluebells and wood anemone.

Just through the trees and around a bend, she found it already shuddering into place: the straight, flat path she had walked with Callum and Iona a year or two before. The corpse road, an ancient funeral route where coffin-bearers had once carried caskets to consecrated ground. The route that would lead her to the Heartwood.

A deep feeling of satisfaction settled in her chest. She had found it.

"Ivy!" said a familiar voice.

She could hardly believe her ears. She spun around, but before she even had a chance to brace, Grendel had leapt up at her, knocking her to the ground, and she was smothered with licks. Ivy fought him off, laughing, and heard kestrel-Callum shriek from the branches overhead.

"It's all right," she called up to him – because emerging from the trees, his face lit up by an infectious grin, was Kit.

"Kit!" she cried out. He met her in a crushing hug and Ivy's heart swelled as she clung to him. When she finally released him he was laughing with his nose all crinkled. She held on to his arm, afraid he might vanish like a mirage.

"You're here," she breathed. Her relief was palpable. She didn't need to wonder what had become of him any more. She didn't need to worry about the way they had parted. He was here. They were back together. He looked tidier, like he too had had a bath and a proper meal and a good night's sleep. His face was fuller, his eyes brighter, and he was happy to see her. That, more than anything, made her feel light as air.

"Is that—?" Kit was saying, and she saw he was looking up into the leafy overstory, where Callum was perched on a branch, eyes flickering over them.

"It's Callum," she supplied, glee glittering in her voice.

Kit's mouth fell open and he stared at her in disbelief. Then he threw an arm around her shoulders and squeezed her. "You found him!" he cheered. "That's amazing!" He stepped away, took another long look at Callum, and shook his head in wonder.

Ivy wasn't quite sure how to ask about Billy when his brother was clearly not with him, so instead she said, "You found Eveling?"

Kit had his hands on his hips now and was turning a slow circle as though orienting himself. He started when his roving gaze fell on the surface of Haweswater, just visible through the trees.

"That's the thing," he said slowly, looking back at her. "I was just there. Grendel and I found him in the ruins of the Roman baths at Glanoventa. I was with him for a day or more, I'm not really sure… He insisted on all of us having picnics and banquets and – well, basically eating all the time. He said the food wouldn't do me any harm, and I was so hungry. It was wonderful – I feel like I never need to eat again. Then he finally summoned me to talk to him and I told him I wanted to see my brother. And then… we were here. And I saw you." He half-smiled, but this time it didn't quite reach his eyes.

Ivy settled down on the forest floor among the bluebells and leaned back on her palms, sensing there was more to the story. Grendel curled up beside her, resting his head on her thigh. Even though Kit's story seemed odd, she felt overwhelmingly grateful that whatever Eveling had intended had somehow brought them back together. "So he granted your wish?" she pressed.

"I think so," Kit said, still casting his eyes around the wood. His shoulders slumped. "But Billy doesn't seem to be here." When he looked at her again, his face was reddening. He crouched down to her level, resting his elbows on his knees, and plucked the head off a bluebell. "I need to tell you something, Ivy. I need to apologise."

Ivy felt her heart pick up speed, not knowing what he could have to be sorry for.

He seemed to steel himself to meet her gaze. "I took the fairy bead," he said.

She felt her eyes go wide. *Kit* had taken it from her?

"After we escaped the flood, I was so angry. I pretended to walk away – but then I followed you to the tower. When you fell asleep, I took it out of your pack… Ivy, I gave it to Eveling. In exchange for my wish. I'm sorry."

Ivy waited a moment for the tide of anger to rise,

but nothing happened. She saw the complex web of emotions that flickered across Kit's face: hurt, guilt, sorrow and hope... Wouldn't she have done the same for Callum?

"It's okay," she said, looking past him. "I was selfish. I wasn't helping you enough. You were right to take it — I still don't know why he wanted me to have it, but I managed to find him without it." And even if she had returned the bead to Taliesin, he had made it clear he couldn't unmake the spell. There was no use being angry, not when she had so much to be sorry for.

Kit's mouth formed a hard line. "I really am sorry."

She reached out a hand and waited for a moment until he took it in his own. His palm was rough, but his fingers were warm as they curled around hers. "I'm sorry too," she said. "I wasn't a good friend to you, but I've kept something from you as well. Something important."

Kit read the expression on her face and sat down heavily on the ground opposite her. "What is it?"

Ivy took a deep breath. She had never really had to explain this to anyone. Everyone in Beckfoot knew what had happened to her; it had made the local news. She hardly knew how to articulate it, but she knew where to begin.

"We used to go fell-walking a lot — me and Callum and my mum. I was good at it. Reading the map, pushing on through the hard parts. I thought I could do anything. One weekend Mum was too busy to take us out, but I was dead set on climbing Irton Fell. I thought

I could just go on my own, but I must have known it was a bad idea really, because I didn't tell Mum. I told Callum where I was going, but I wouldn't take him with me. He was mad about that.

"I didn't know I'd forgotten the map. I was out for hours and hours. I reached the top and I was so happy with myself, but on the way down I came off the path somewhere and got lost. Nothing was familiar and the trees were so dense I couldn't see where I was. I kept walking around, trying to find a path and getting more and more stressed, and then – I caught my foot on a root and fell. It snapped my ankle.

"I screamed and screamed, but no one could hear me. I had a panic attack. I couldn't breathe… I thought I was going to die. Eventually it passed, but by that time it was dark. I spent the night on the fell, alone. My ankle hurt so much, and I was exhausted from the walk and the panic attack. I was so scared…"

Kit didn't say anything, but he watched her with total focus.

Ivy cleared her throat and carried on. "They had Mountain Rescue out looking for me. But it was Mum who found me, at five o'clock in the morning. She'd been walking all night and most of the day before, ever since Callum had told her where I'd gone. I was airlifted to the hospital, and they fixed my ankle and put it in a cast. It healed fine after a couple of months. But I haven't been… myself, since."

She found that cold tears were flowing slowly down

her cheeks. "I can't go into the fells any more. If I don't know the way, if I can't see the path I need, I just – lose it. I have to take my map everywhere with me. Had to, I mean." Her voice cracked. "I can't even walk to school on my own, and it's only around the corner. Callum wants to go out exploring. I can tell he does, but Mum wants me to feel comfortable, so they don't go out without me much."

She wiped the tears away and sniffed. "I'm sorry I didn't tell you."

Kit shuffled over so that he was sitting beside her, then put an arm around her shoulders. "I don't care," he said. "Ivy, I would hardly have known. All right, I noticed you were very attached to your map, but I can't believe you've done all this for Callum! And you've been leading the way this whole time. I could barely put one foot in front of the other when we split up. I was amazed we found Eveling at all!"

She laughed at that, and he met her eyes and grinned. "And you've found Callum!" he added, gesturing to the silent bird of prey who had been watching the whole exchange.

"He *is* still a kestrel, though," Ivy said, quiet enough that she hoped Callum wouldn't overhear.

Kit rolled his eyes. "Not for long, I'm sure. Come on then, what's the plan? What are you doing here?"

He jumped to his feet, holding out a hand. Ivy gently pushed Grendel off her legs and took it, hauling herself up.

"I was going to follow the corpse road south-east to a

place called the Heartwood, because, well, the birds told me to... Even when he had no reason to lie, Taliesin still said he couldn't undo the spell. I don't know what will be there, but at this point, it's my only hope." She paused. "But what do you want to do? The most important thing is that we stick together."

Kit turned to look at the open, grassy path that lay ahead of them. "I don't know. Maybe Eveling was playing a trick on me, sending me back to this valley in search of Billy. Or maybe I'm meant to go with you. I thought that our paths were diverging, but here we are."

Ivy hit him in the shoulder. "You don't have to sound so happy about it," she laughed.

He shrugged her off with a smile. "Come on, then. Let's get going."

The Corpse Road

OS Grid Ref: NY 49 12

They left the shelter of the woodland and set out along the corpse road: Ivy, Kit and Grendel on foot, Callum flying low overhead. On one side the lush green fells rolled up towards the not-sky, and on the other the valley flowed down to the periwinkle surface of the reservoir.

Grendel trotted ahead, his tail wagging non-stop. Kit had his neck craned back to watch Callum flying, an awestruck smile on his face. Ivy kept stealing glances at her friend, unable to believe her luck in finding him again. When he caught her staring he gave her a friendly shove.

But when she looked back at the trail, she jolted in surprise. There was a woman walking along the path towards them.

"Kit," Ivy said under her breath. "There's someone coming."

He glanced ahead and laughed. "So? They don't have wings, you don't need to worry."

"That's my point. All this time, we've never passed a single other human just walking along like us. So it *is* a bit weird, thank you very much."

The woman in question was closing in on them now. She wore a long blue dress and a cloak over her shoulders; her copper hair was piled on top of her head, and there was a golden torc around her neck. Her brow was knitted in worry.

Ivy wasn't sure what hiking etiquette was in Underfell, but she ventured a polite "Hello!"

The woman seemed not to hear her. They had to jump out of her way to avoid being barrelled through.

Kit raised his eyebrows at Ivy. "Rude."

They continued on in the shadow of the kestrel. Ivy began to fill Kit in on her adventures since they had parted ways, so neither of them noticed the other travellers approaching until they were upon them.

"Excuse us," said an imperious voice, making Ivy jump.

She and Kit stepped off the path to allow a group of men to pass. All three wore baggy trousers tucked into long socks, and carried jute rucksacks hung with heavy hooks and coils of rope. They looked exactly like the bearded climbers in the old photos that hung in Beckfoot's village pub. The men strode quickly past, nodding hello.

As they stepped back onto the trail, Ivy did a double take. She had to glance at Kit to check he was seeing the same thing she was. There was a bemused smile on his face now, and the beginnings of concern in his brow.

The path was becoming busier still. Ahead of them, two pale men with smart velvet jackets and white cravats ambled along with a woman wearing a bonnet and a dress with a puffy skirt. They paused to admire a patch of daffodils at the side of the road.

A whole troop of men and women with long braided hair and what looked like armour made of stiff leather were marching purposefully down the path. Ivy was startled to realise they had swords and axes strapped to their backs and hips.

Strangest of all, though, was that there was not a pair of wings in sight.

In all this time, they had encountered less than a handful of humans in Underfell. Yet here they all were. It gave Ivy a distinct feeling of unease.

More climbers passed, some clad in modern waterproofs and harnesses, others looking totally out of time. People with faces darkened by soot began shambling past, some carrying lanterns, others wearing head torches – miners. There were children among them, coughing and coated in dirt.

A disparate troop of men moved past them, ancient soldiers with shining armour and plumed helmets. But their faces were clouded, and the *SPQR* banner one man bore was torn and flapped forgotten in his wake.

The travellers were passing in both directions, some at a fast clip, others stopping every so often as they shuffled by, looking around in confusion. Some greeted

Kit and Ivy as they passed, but others seemed too distressed to even notice them.

"Where are they all going?" Kit asked quietly.

A teenage girl with tightly braided black hair cantered by bareback on a draft horse, face troubled.

"I don't know," Ivy murmured, though even as she said it, she began to wonder.

A steady stream of boys and men had begun to appear over the hill, flowing down into the valley. They all wore variants of the same tattered green uniform, with tarnished buttons and muddy black boots. Some of them levered themselves forwards on crutches; on others, one sleeve hung empty from their shoulders. There were women amongst them in stained white aprons with red crosses.

There was something frighteningly familiar about these scenes. Ivy had seen pictures just like them in her school history textbook – in the pages about the First World War.

"BILLY!"

Kit's voice suddenly erupted beside her. She turned to him and saw that his face was flushed and bright.

"What is it?" she asked, following his line of sight. He didn't even seem to hear her.

"Billy!" he shouted again, pushing forward through the throng of people.

When Ivy searched the crowd this time she spotted him almost at once, because the young man looked just like a version of Kit that had been stretched out by a growth spurt, with gaunter cheeks, longer limbs and a slightly bigger nose. He was wearing the same muddied uniform as the rest of the men, marching slowly along the road with an unfocused gaze.

Ivy's heart stopped. For a moment she couldn't move.

Then she pushed her way through the crowd after Kit, grabbing onto the back of his jumper, keeping as close to him as she could.

"Billy, it's me!" As Kit's voice cut over the crowd something flickered in his brother's face, but it vanished as quickly as it had come, and the soldier didn't change course.

"Billy!" Kit called again, his voice cracking.

This time, his brother's head turned. Billy's eyes seemed to pass over Kit in slow motion, then his blank expression gradually creased into a broad smile. "Kit!" he said delightedly. "Is that you?!"

"Billy, I've been looking for you for – for bloody ages! Where have you been?"

Kit was laughing, but there seemed to be more people moving along the road than ever. Ivy was pressed into Kit's back by the throng, and Grendel was quickly lost in the sea of legs. Callum trilled overhead; there was an edge of distress to the sound.

"I've been in France, you idiot! Where'd you think?" Billy replied with teasing roughness. Yet though his focus was on Kit, his legs kept propelling him onwards.

Kit tried to find a way to close the gap between them, but there always seemed to be someone in the way.

"After you helped me climb Castle Crag, where'd you go? I followed you!"

Billy frowned. He looked as though he was striving to recover a memory that wasn't there. "I don't know," he said, and then his eyes glazed over again.

Kit shook his head. "Come on," he said firmly. "We've got to get you home. Mam and Dad'll be over the moon to see you." He gave one valiant push and emerged at his brother's side. Billy laughed and threw his arms around his brother, holding him tight, patting him firmly on the back.

But then his arms fell away as he began to move again, very slowly, taking steps along the road back the way Kit and Ivy had come.

"We're going this way." Kit tugged on his brother's sleeve to pull him in the other direction. "Come on. We just have to make one stop and then we'll go home."

Billy's eyes flickered back from the road to Kit, as though he had forgotten his brother was there. "I can't," he said, and though his voice was distant there was an edge of pain to it.

"What do you mean?" asked Kit, his brow wrinkling in distress. "Where are you going?"

Billy's head turned back in the direction the others were moving. The tide, surging onwards, of soldiers and miners and climbers and sailors and farmers and shepherds and children.

"Follow the road," Billy answered, but it was like he was speaking from a dream.

Ivy remembered Iona telling them stories as they

walked along the corpse road, creeping up and grabbing their shoulders to spook them, all three of them falling about laughing. About how before every village had a graveyard, people would travel this road with the coffins of their loved ones, carrying them long distances through the fells to bury them beside a church.

Ivy understood with dawning certainty why there were people here from all corners of Cumbrian history, of all ages, dressed as though they had just stepped out of their own time.

"Kit." She reached forward to squeeze his arm, trying to somehow get his attention. He shook her off and she lost her grip on the back of his jumper. Before she had a chance to think, other people had pressed in between them, gently shifting the two of them apart as they moved on their way.

"Kit!" she called again. He must have heard the note of panic in her voice because he turned, then seemed startled to find they were being separated. "I'm sorry," Ivy choked out, lifting her voice, not knowing how to express what she must. "Kit… Kit, he's dead."

Kit's eyes first went wide, then narrowed, and he gave his head a shake as if to dislodge her words. He turned back to his brother, only to discover that Billy had passed him by and was moving away along the road. "Billy!" he shouted, making an effort to push back the way they'd come, but the dead prevented him.

Billy seemed to have a sudden rush of strength and he held out his hand over the shoulders of the crowd. Kit clasped it in his, though the surge of the surrounding people was already prising them apart.

"I'm sorry, Kit," Billy said. There were tears in his eyes. "I'm sorry I won't be there."

The momentum of the crowd pulled their fingers apart, and Kit's face crumpled.

"Tell Mam and Dad I love 'em," Billy called back to him. "I love you all. Tell 'em!"

Just like that, all the fight went out of Kit, and he let himself be pushed to the edge of the road, passers-by bumping roughly against his shoulders. Ivy felt herself nudged aside with him, letting out a deep breath as she was expelled from the crowd.

"I'll tell them," Kit replied in a small voice that was swallowed up by the sound of shuffling footsteps.

Billy kept looking back at his brother even as he was hurried onwards, until finally his uniformed figure became indistinguishable in the mob of retreating soldiers. There were others among them now, with different helmets and berets, trailing half-opened parachutes, shouldering different kinds of weapons.

At last the crowd thinned enough for Grendel to come running back to them. Kit was still staring off in the direction his brother had disappeared, looking lost.

Ivy closed the gap between them and wrapped him into a hug. His arms hung limply by his sides, and she pressed her face into his shoulder. "I'm sorry, Kit," she mumbled. "I'm so sorry."

He was silent for a long time. Finally, he whispered,

"He can't be dead," and began to sob.

That sorrowful sound was all it took to open the floodgates and send tears streaming down Ivy's face as well. She tried not to make a sound, but her shoulders shook as she held Kit close, letting his tears soak into her hair. She felt strangely numb, like her body was reacting while her mind still struggled to grasp the truth.

When at last she felt like she could face Kit without sobbing, she unwound her arms, wiped the tears off his face, and squeezed his hand. He just stood there, his face wet, staring unseeing at his boots. Grendel, who had been sitting nearby, got up and came over to lick Kit's free hand entreatingly.

It was Grendel who finally got them moving by setting off along the corpse road as though he intended to continue without them. Kit began to follow, setting one foot after the other. Ivy was pulled along with him, and eventually their hands untangled.

They reached the end of the corpse road when it ran under an iron gate into a churchyard. There was no building within, only rows of moss-covered, weathered gravestones. Just over the brow of the hill, Ivy knew they would find the valley of the Heartwood. But for now, the not-sky was darkening to a rich shade of aubergine, and it was time to make camp.

She fed Grendel, who bolted down his pink kibble gratefully. Callum flew to her arm and she told him that they would be resting for the night. She wasn't sure how much he understood, but he flew to the lowest branch of a nearby oak and hunched himself up as if ready for sleep.

Ivy found that she didn't feel like zipping herself into the cocoon of her tent tonight; instead, she folded the groundsheet into a long rectangle and lay down on that. She passed Kit the sleeping bag, but he didn't get in either, just lay it out nearby and stretched out on top of it, hands pillowed under his head. There was something companionable about lying under the glowing canopy side by side, not separated by the walls of a tent.

As she tried in vain to fall asleep, Ivy felt a wave of rage and frustration building inside her until her body seemed to hum with the injustice of it all. Kit had come here looking for his brother just like she had, and had found him only to lose him again. He had searched for a hundred years. He had watched his home and his village drown. He had done everything he could to help Ivy, and he had still lost his brother.

He seemed to be sleeping now, so she let the tears that kept creeping up on her spill down the sides of her face.

Underfell was a magical place, but that did not mean it was kind.

What would happen when they finally passed through the wall again? Would Ivy be bringing another wayward soul back to Beckfoot and Iona? Or would Kit somehow find his way home to bring the news to his parents?

All Ivy could do was make sure that Kit made it back to Cumbria one way or another, and that neither of them would walk out of here alone.

Heartwood

OS Grid Ref: NY 61 00

Ivy and Kit strode up to the crest of the hill the following morning, a border collie racing around their heels and a kestrel soaring high over their heads.

They peered down into a broad valley, traced through by a steady river and dotted with farms. The fellsides that rolled up from the riverbank were criss-crossed with drystone walls chasing right up to their peaks. As Ivy swept her gaze over it, she envisioned the wide motorway she remembered winding along the side of the hill, the train tracks below.

At once she felt her error. The ground began to quake beneath them, and soon it was shaking so violently that they had to crouch down or lose their balance. Ivy watched in awe as several lanes of tarmac erupted from the ground and began ironing themselves out, punctuated by dashes of white paint. Railway sleepers shot out of the soil and arranged themselves in rows, interlinked by steel rails, until the train line ran right through the valley and out of sight.

When the dust had settled Kit just stared at the road. "Is that real?"

It was the first thing he'd said all morning.

"I'm sorry." Ivy winced. "I forgot…"

But Kit was already pushing himself up to his feet. Without a word he jogged down the slope and stopped at the edge. He stepped out onto the tarmac.

"Look both ways!" Ivy yelled, clambering to her feet to race after him. Even as she said it, she realised it wouldn't matter. The very idea of cars in Underfell was jarring.

But here was the motorway. And she had revealed it.

Kit was looking up and down the road, walking in a wide circle in the centre of it, like he was taking the first steps on the moon. He had a hand over his mouth and his brow was heavy.

Ivy walked out after him, fighting her instincts to make herself step onto the tarmac.

"This is from your time?" Kit asked, lowering his hand.

"Yeah."

He squeezed his eyes shut, reaching at the same time for the loose watch on his wrist. He twisted it around and around. Looking at it now, Ivy could see that the reason the watch had looked so peculiar was because it was old, a wind-up pocket watch on a fraying strap. It was an antique, a piece of history.

"Billy gave it to me," he told her, and she saw that he had opened his eyes and was watching her. "The last time he came home."

Ivy's mouth began to form the words *I'm so sorry*, but she stopped herself, pressing her lips together. She searched desperately for the words to comfort a boy who might be about to lose a century, on top of everything else.

"It's a good watch," she said.

Kit was worrying his lower lip with his teeth, but then he heaved a great sigh and dropped his hand. "Will this road take us to the wood?"

Ivy led the way. She walked down the middle of the mammoth, empty road; it was eerie, but strangely liberating.

They came around a curve in the hillside and there it was, facing them like a painting displayed on a wall. The Heartwood was little more than a copse, hardly large enough to be called a wood. In full leaf, the foliage created the shape of a heart, rough but impossible to miss, whether by chance or intention, no one seemed to know.

She felt a tugging from her chest down to her toes, like her feet were sending down roots into the earth, holding her steady. It was the way she always felt when she saw the heart-shaped wood from the train or the car as she travelled home after time away.

The wood had a palpable presence. It seemed to hum and vibrate. *Strong magic*, Ivy heard herself thinking.

She closed her eyes and listened to the chorus of birds flitting overhead, hopping over the ground, perched in the branches of trees. She let the word wash over her.

Heartwood, Heartwood, Heartwood.

"Is that where we're going?" Kit asked.

Ivy nodded. "For better or worse." She looked at him and swallowed. "Kit—"

"We'll see this through together," he said, meeting her eyes. "And then we'll go home. All of us."

Her heart swelled with gratitude that she had had the unlikely good fortune to find Kit so early in her journey, and that he was choosing to stay with her even now, when he had lost everything he had been searching for.

Ivy stepped from the road into the long grass, looking ahead to trace their route through the valley to the wood. The grass was alight with flowers and thrumming with insects and small creatures. She held herself still and let the untrodden valley fill her vision, soaking it in. There was not a path in sight; the world was wide open before her.

She would not be weighed down by it. She was buoyed up by it.

As they approached the wood, the birds stopped singing. The change was so sudden that the silence that followed rang in Ivy's ears. She could hear their footsteps clearly, the running of the river below them, the breaking of twigs in the woods ahead – but not a single bird.

When they reached the treeline, there was a shift in the quality of the air.

"Can you feel that?" she asked under her breath.

"Like before a storm," Kit answered. The air felt

charged and heavy; walking began to feel more like wading. The handprint on Ivy's arm started to prickle uncomfortably.

Up close, the wall of trees loomed over them, dense as a thicket of thorns. Ivy led the way along its edge for a time before she found a gap large enough to admit them. She ducked under a branch and squeezed in among the close trunks, pushing aside low-hanging branches and stepping carefully through the tangle of thick, raised roots.

The trees here were ancient: gnarled, long-fingered oaks; sweet chestnuts with twisted trunks; fluted yews with probing branches. Progress was slow as they picked their way between them. Grendel padded along at the rear, uncharacteristically hesitant. Callum moved silently from branch to branch in short bursts; the dense woodland gave him no room to glide.

A flutter of wings caught Ivy's eye and she stopped. Perched in the clinging branches of a hawthorn, half-hidden among the red berries, was a hawfinch.

A chirp – and there was another one: a splash of gold and silver, brown and black. Dozens more were settling into the canopy above, undisturbed by the kestrel swooping between the boughs beneath them.

It couldn't be. It wasn't possible. He had already told her there was nothing he could do. But these were *his* birds.

It was nothing more than a coincidence. It had to be.

A strong gust of wind sprang up out of nowhere,

whipping at their clothes and hair and fur. The leaning trees groaned against it, but when it subsided, the groan only grew louder. The prickling sensation in Ivy's arm became so intense it was almost painful. She looked back at Kit, who was still braced against the wind, clutching one wrist. Grendel was shrunk low against the ground. Ivy felt her heartbeat accelerate as the leaves began to tremble with the growing sound, and gradually, it took the shape of words.

"*WHO ENTERS MY RESTING PLACE?*"

The voice was so loud that it beat at Ivy's eardrums; the wood resonated with it. All the hawfinches took off at once and began flying frantically in circles overhead. The ground beneath them began to tremble: *BOOM, BOOM*, like colossal footsteps. Gold and emerald leaves showered down on them from above.

"*WHO DISTURBS THEIR KING?*" the voice thundered.

All at once the soil ahead of them erupted. Trees were shoved aside as the ground roiled and cracked. At first all Ivy could see was a misshapen crown of unpolished gold, scratched and tarnished. Its bearer was a giant five times as large as anyone she had seen before, his long hair white, his eyes huge and sunken. His papery skin, the colour of stoneware, told of centuries.

It was the Spectre King, but not as she knew him.

Kit grabbed Ivy's arm. Grendel crouched with his tail between his legs. The ancient king pulled himself up to his full, uncanny height, stared right at them, then pointed a long, bony finger at Ivy. She went cold.

All the hawfinches dove at once. Ivy, Kit and Grendel were surrounded in a heartbeat by a flurry of wings and claws and beaks pecking and scratching and tearing at their hair. Somewhere overhead, Callum was screeching. Ivy's arms flew up to shield her face, and she threw herself down over Grendel.

"URIEN!"

A terrified voice sliced through the shrieking of the hawfinches, and just like that, the onslaught ceased. Ivy gasped for breath as the birds withdrew and Kit sank to his knees beside her.

She knew that voice. She was so *tired* of that voice.

Taliesin was standing in the trees at the edge of the clearing that the king's eruption had created. His tie was loosened, his shirt sleeves rolled up, and his arms were full of firewood. He was frozen, staring in horror at the giant ghost king in the centre of the chaos.

The spectre collapsed.

Taliesin dropped his armful of wood with a clatter, threw out his wings and soared across the clearing. On the ground lay a man who was tall, but a giant no longer. The lines in his face suggested he might be in his fifties, and the hair of his uncrowned head was silver-grey and cropped short.

There was no doubting that this was the same ghostly monarch who had pursued her across Underfell. But the last of Ivy's fear melted away at the sight of the crumpled man on the forest floor.

Was this woodland Taliesin's home? Had he sent the Spectre King after them from the start? Why would the birds bring her here, of all places? Questions rushed through her mind as she steeled herself and slowly approached.

Taliesin was gently shaking the man's shoulder, tapping his face.

"Urien," he murmured. "Wake up. Wake up."

The man came round with a deep breath, blinking sleepily. "What happened?" he asked in a soft voice.

Taliesin didn't answer him, but instead turned his face towards Ivy, not meeting her gaze. "Did you find the fairy bead?" he asked.

"No," said Ivy.

Taliesin shut his eyes tight. "Then you should go." He pulled Urien bodily to his feet, slung one of the man's arms around his shoulders, and began to lead him away.

Ivy hesitated for a moment before following. "Can't you just make another one?" she pressed.

"No," Taliesin replied through gritted teeth. "I'm not going to explain a lifetime of magical teachings to a child, but the bead your brother stole was an important piece of a very old spell which *cannot be remade*."

He stopped before an aged oak tree that towered over all the others. There was a roughly hewn door set into a great hollow at its base, the sort of thing Ivy would doodle while daydreaming. Taliesin seemed to be trying to work out how he could open the door while supporting Urien, but Kit darted forwards to open it for him.

Begrudgingly, Taliesin stepped through, Urien leaning heavily against him. Ivy quickly followed, beckoning to Kit to come with her, and Grendel padded in at their heels. Kestrel-Callum remained outside, watching curiously from the boughs above.

There was an earthy smell in the dark stairway that wound down from the hollow trunk into the ground beneath. Amber light glowed from the foot of the stair, where they found themselves in a spacious, round chamber. Its walls were packed earth, run through with roots as thick as beams. There was a handmade bed, a kitchen and table, and a cosy area with sheepskin rugs and pelts and armchairs around the hearth. The walls were hung with framed sketches and antlers and colourful leaves. It was a home.

Taliesin settled Urien into one of the armchairs. The man's eyes were still half-closed, and he took in the room with a look of vague confusion. Ivy stood back with the others, giving them space.

"We didn't know you would be here," she said quietly. "The birds told us to come. I just thought it might be something that could break the spell."

"Your brother stole from me, you lied to me, and now the fairy bead is gone." Taliesin ground out the words. "You won't find help here."

"Callum didn't steal from you!" Ivy snapped, tired of this old refrain. "He wouldn't have taken it without good reason. If you unmake the spell maybe we can ask him!"

"You know why the boy wanted it, Tal," said a slow, steady voice. They all looked to Urien in surprise. He took a deep breath; his eyes were weary when he met Ivy's gaze. "The bead is not Taliesin's. It is mine. A protection charm."

He held up his arm and Ivy saw that wrapped around his wrist and forearm was a long string of stone beads, identical in shape and size to the one Callum had given her, but all the colours of the sky and the fells and the water.

"The boy came here looking for a protection charm for his sister," Urien went on, though speaking seemed to require great effort. "He was worried about her. He said she had been afraid for a long time. And he wanted to help." He turned his gaze on Taliesin, whose face was etched with bewilderment. "He didn't steal the bead, Tal. I gave it to him."

"What?" The word came out in a gasp. Taliesin dropped to his knees in front of Urien.

Ivy stepped back towards Kit, feeling suddenly intrusive.

Urien reached out and took Taliesin's hand in both of his, stroking it with his thumbs. "You know this can't go on much longer," he said. "It's been over a thousand years. I'm human. I'm not made to survive in a place like this. Not for this long."

"No," Taliesin protested quietly.

"Look at what happened today," Urien continued in a level voice. "I attacked children! I can't control the magic any more. It's changing me, you know it is. It's

258

taken its toll… and I'm so very tired."

Taliesin was shaking his head. "You need to be ready. For when you're needed again in Rheged. You're their king."

It was as though the two men had forgotten they had any company at all. Ivy glanced over at Kit, but he was staring raptly at the scene.

"The world has moved on, Tal. Cumbria doesn't need a king any more," Urien said. He turned his head, met Ivy's eye, and smiled.

"But why did you follow us?" she asked, struggling to reconcile the spectre that had haunted her journey with this kind man's smile. "Why did you attack me?"

The lines on his face shifted in confusion. "What do you mean?"

"At the tup fair – you appeared out of nowhere and chased me! And again at Mardale Green, when the village was flooding—"

"And at Glanoventa, right before Eveling appeared," Kit interjected, startling Ivy. "When I was searching the ruins, you were following me. I tried to run away, but you caught me by the wrist and wouldn't let go. And then you just vanished." His face had turned pale at the memory, and he rolled up the cuff of his sleeve to reveal a silver handprint, just like Ivy's, clenched around his right wrist. Ivy's mouth fell open.

"I didn't see him after Mardale Green," she said to Kit. "He went with you." Understanding was beginning to dawn.

Taliesin closed his eyes as though in exasperation. "At Glanoventa, I don't suppose you had the fairy bead with you, did you, Christopher?"

Kit swallowed. "Um—"

"Oh, children. I'm so sorry," Urien interrupted, rubbing his temples. "When I gave Callum the bead, I didn't consider… You must have been so frightened…"

Taliesin laid a hand over Urien's, but when he spoke, it was to Ivy and Kit. "Powerful spellworks, when divided, can sometimes carry a… a trace of their subject," he explained. "An echo."

"Like a ghost," Ivy said.

"It might look like that," Taliesin conceded. "A footprint of the soul it has been attached to. All it would want – it wouldn't *want* anything, of course, but its purpose – would be to see the spellwork reunited. It would have taken the bead from you if it could, and brought it back to us. But it couldn't." He looked uneasily from Ivy's arm to Kit's, to the shimmering shadows of a spectral hand.

Then he turned his back on them, taking hold of both of Urien's hands. "If Eveling has it, we may be able to bargain with him to get it back," he said urgently.

Urien was already shaking his head. "Tal. Don't make this harder than it needs to be."

Ivy drew in a breath, feeling like an intruder again. Taliesin must have heard her because he leapt to his feet and whirled around. "How many times do I have to tell you to get out of here?" he shouted. "This is a private matter. I can't help you!"

"You have to!" Ivy protested. "I can't do it without you."

"You can," said Urien. His voice had grown in strength, and he pushed himself up straighter.

"How?" she asked helplessly. "Taliesin made the spell with his anger, so he has to be the one to unmake it."

"Yes, he was angry," said Urien. "These beads are all that keep me alive, and when he saw that one was gone, he was worried. He knew it would make me more fragile. But a part of him was also relieved. I know I'm right, Tal. He was relieved, as I was, that part of the decision had been made for us. We knew it was my time. He still fought to keep the charm intact, but he did not have the fury he needed to stop your brother, who was already far away. Are you going to tell her?"

This last remark was directed at Taliesin, who had been watching Ivy throughout this speech, cringing, but never taking his eyes off her. He sighed deeply.

"I felt something much stronger," he said at last. "I felt the dismay, and frustration, and self-loathing of a girl whose brother was calling for her help, who could not bring herself to go to his aid."

Ivy felt like the wind had been knocked out of her. "You used *my* feelings?" she said breathlessly. "My feelings made Callum… into… a bird?" She could barely string the sentence together.

The room seemed to lose focus; everything took on that dreaded tinge of grey. She was aware that the others were still speaking, but she couldn't seem to hear anything they said.

It was *her*. Her failure. She hadn't helped Callum, and in failing to do so, she had allowed all this to happen.

And then, as quickly as it had come, the grey fog cleared. The sounds in the room sharpened.

Ivy thought of Bega, who had fled from Ireland in turmoil, and inadvertently transformed herself into a seal. It wasn't until she let go of her anger and guilt – and forgave herself for leaving everything behind – that she became a woman again…

As Ivy turned and sprinted up the winding stair, she was only dimly aware of the others following. She burst out into the pale fuchsia light of the wood and threw up her fist.

"Callum North!"

Her forearm moved with the kestrel's momentum as he collided with her. She lifted her free hand to stroke the feathers under his beak. She was not certain whether it was Callum or the bird looking out of those black eyes, but she had to try.

She opened her mouth to apologise to him, then closed it again. What had Taliesin said? Her self-loathing was the catalyst he had used for the spellwork. That was what had got them into this mess.

Since that first moment when fear had prevented her from helping her brother, Ivy had done everything in her power to find Callum. She had come into this strange place alone. She had hiked miles upon miles, back and forth across the landscape, in search of the answers to unmake the spell. She had woken an ancient witch from stone; travelled through the sky on a flying pony; survived the sinking of Mardale Green; walked a mile in a mine beneath the sea. She had found her way in a realm where the paths had minds of their own and banished the grey fog.

"You'll need to craft something for the counter-spellwork," said Urien from the doorway, where he was leaning. Taliesin stood beneath the trees, and Kit was only a few steps behind her, a smile on his lips. Even Grendel sat watching.

"Is there something you can make?" Taliesin offered. "Can you sing?"

Ivy picked up a birch twig and held it poised over the soil and leaf litter. "I make maps," she said firmly.

As she retraced her steps in her mind, she sketched the landscape onto the ground. Here was the sleeping woodland where she had first met Kit; there was Mayburgh Henge, where Bega had come to her aid. Here was the falconer's tower; there the Refuge; Mardale Green and Saltom Pit and Long Meg with her many daughters. As she drew, she felt a swelling of pride for everything she had achieved. The feeling pooled in her feet and filled her up, glowing gold as sunshine. It reached her fingertips just as she sketched the final 'X' – home.

Ivy felt her arm growing heavier, and she threw up her fist for the kestrel to take wing – but as it left her, those wings became arms, and those feathers became the messy hair of a nine-year-old boy...

And Callum landed with a thump on his feet.

Two Spells Woven

OS Grid Ref: NY 61 00

Callum straightened up, grinning, and Ivy burst into tears.

She grabbed her brother and pulled him to her. Somehow she was laughing and crying at the same time, and when she looked at Kit she saw he was crying too, and she flung out an arm and drew him into the hug. Grendel was barking and jumping all over them, covering their clothes in dirty pawprints.

"You did well, Ivy," Kit murmured into her hair.

Over their heads, she saw that Taliesin and Urien were standing together in the doorway. Their hands were clasped, and the fairy's forehead was pressed against the human king's shoulder.

"I've got SO MUCH to tell you!" Callum wriggled free of their embrace. "I can't believe it. I was a kestrel! YOU turned me into a kestrel!" He spun around, pointing at Taliesin.

The fairy raised his head and shifted uncomfortably. "It was a misunderstanding—" he began to say, but

Callum was already running around the clearing with his arms flung wide.

"I got to FLY!"

"That's wonderful," Ivy replied, embarrassed to find that there was no stemming the tide of her tears.

"Why don't you tell us all about it over dinner?" Urien suggested gently. "We have plenty of human food here. Taliesin's developed quite a taste for it, haven't you, Tal?"

Kit quickly wiped his own cheeks with the back of a hand and sniffed. "You know, I think I'm finally starting to get my appetite back." He patted his belly. As they followed Taliesin back into the tree-root house, he added, "We had a taste of flying too, didn't we, Ivy?"

"I tried to forget about that, actually." Ivy covered her face with a hand.

"You flew?" Callum looked back at them in wonder.

"On a horse," Kit said, delighting in his excitement. "Peregrine, the legendary fell pony."

"Peregrine?" Urien repeated, stopping on the stairs. His face was alight. "My Peregrine? You saw her?"

"She gave us a lift to meet Taliesin," Ivy explained.

Urien practically glowed as Taliesin guided him the rest of the way down the stairs and settled him back into his armchair.

"Do you realise what that means? *He's* the king from the story!" Kit murmured to Ivy, awestruck.

Callum launched himself onto the soft pile of animal pelts beside the fire. Kit ended up peeling potatoes with

Taliesin, looking slightly unsure of himself, but Ivy felt that the fairy's whole demeanour had changed. Taliesin's posture was more relaxed, and his voice was gentler. Even if he did seem melancholy and distracted, it was undoubtedly an improvement on the threatening mayor of Saltom Pit.

Ivy filled the kettle and brought it over to the hearth to hang above the fire. She settled herself down beside her brother while the water heated.

"Callum, I think we need to get some things worked out," she said. "How long were you in Underfell before I saw you through the wall?"

He was lying on his back on the pelts, and he tilted his head so she was looking at him upside down. "I dunno. A day?"

"A day?" If she had been drinking at that moment, she would have spat it across the room. "What do you mean, a day?"

Callum shrugged. "Travelling's different, isn't it? When I came through the wall I spoke to a chaffinch and said I was looking for some magic to help you be brave. Then all the birds started telling me to go to the Heartwood, so I came straight here. I talked to Urien and he gave me one of his beads, and that was that. I headed home again."

Ivy, Kit and Taliesin were all staring at him open-mouthed, but Urien only chuckled at the memory.

"You understood the birds straight away?" Ivy asked, incredulous.

Callum made a silly face. "Didn't you?"

Ivy shook her head in disbelief. "We have a lot to talk about when we get home."

"I wonder why the birds were trying to help you?" Kit mused, dropping a peeled potato into a bowl.

"I can answer that," said Taliesin, chopping onions at his side. "Wild animals pass freely between our world and yours. They know where all the doors are, you see. Up above, Ivy and Callum are known as bird-friends: always taking an interest in them, putting seed out, helping when they're injured. Bird-friends are very highly regarded among the avian population in Underfell, which is why they took it upon themselves to help you. Even my finches knew of it. But their loyalty lies... with me." He went a bit quiet at the end.

"But I couldn't understand anything when I was a kestrel," Callum said. "Not the other birds, not people either... That's why I decided to stay put at the Bowder Stone in the end. Wait for you to come to me. I knew you would."

Ivy felt a lump rise in her throat.

"Tell us what it was like being a kestrel, Callum."

But while he recounted his bird's-eye view of his days in Underfell, Ivy found that she hardly heard his words at all. She was too wrapped up in watching her animated little brother: his cackling laughter, his flickering gaze and the broad smile that lit up his face.

Later, they sat around the dining table, tucking into a steaming vegetable stew with freshly baked bread rolls and, of course, tea. Callum ploughed through his meal at Ivy's side, his legs swinging. Urien cleared his throat and began to speak.

"I think you children deserve the full story, if you would like to hear it." He glanced around the table, and when no one raised an objection, he continued. "A long time ago, I was the ruler of the kingdom of Rheged – what's now known as Cumbria. Taliesin travelled to my court to become my bard, but in time we became a great deal more to each other. Tal confided in me that he was not of our world, that he was a fairy, from Underfell. You see, fairies may walk in our world, but no human can see their wings. I learned that Tal would never age or die, as I inevitably would. And when that time came, Taliesin brought me here and crafted these fairy beads as a spellwork to prolong my life indefinitely."

"So that one day he could return to lead his kingdom again," Taliesin interjected.

Urien nudged Taliesin's arm with his elbow. "So that we could stay together," he corrected. "But human beings are not meant to live as long a life as this. I become less myself every day. My memory of the past is patchy, and the present is sometimes unclear too. I can get lost in thought for a minute and discover I've been sitting several hours in one place. I've known for a long time that this cannot go on, but it was only when young Callum here found me and asked for a spell to help his

269

sister that I was compelled to act."

"It shouldn't have worked," Taliesin said, shaking his head.

"I hoped the combination of the bead and Callum's determination might be enough in itself," said Urien. "A brother crossing a fairy realm to find a magical object for his older sister. How could she not be brave after a thing like that? The plan he crafted to aid you, Ivy, was almost perfect – except for the Tal factor." He grinned at his partner.

"That reminds me," Taliesin said. "Ivy, Kit. Would you hold out your arms?"

Intrigued, but still with a flutter of apprehension, Ivy extended her arm with the silver handprint uppermost. Kit did the same. Taliesin leaned across the table to close a hand over each of them, then began to hum and sing. The music held Ivy spellbound as her forearm began to tingle. The feeling grew until she felt like her whole arm was buzzing with pins and needles: then, just like that, it was over. When Taliesin withdrew his hand, the skin of her forearm was unmarked. It was as though the handprint had never been.

"Two spells woven into the same stone: one ancient, one new." Taliesin shook his head. "No wonder the echo couldn't truly touch you."

Ivy squeezed Callum's knee. He squirmed away from her, just like always.

There was a moment of quiet as they savoured their meal. Ivy could still feel the warm glow of magic in her chest from her counter-spellwork.

As they polished off the stew it occurred to her that it had been a long time since Kit had spoken. Even though he had professed his hunger, his bowl was still full, and he only seemed to be nudging the vegetables around with a spoon.

She wasn't the only one to notice.

"Kit," Taliesin said, and set down his cutlery. "When I sent you both to Mardale Green, I had no idea what had become of Billy. I'm so dreadfully sorry." There were crinkles of regret around his eyes, but he held Kit's gaze.

Kit shook his head, looking down at his plate. "Nowt you could have done about it." A moment passed before he continued, "Do you know how it works, getting in and out of this place? How much time will have passed? Will I be a hundred years too late to tell my parents?" On the last question his voice cracked, and he swallowed.

Taliesin looked troubled. "It's hard to say," he admitted. "Sometimes when I pass through a door, I find it's only been half an hour since I was last in Rheged. On other occasions, I find I've missed decades."

Kit nodded solemnly. Ivy laid down her spoon and reached across the table to cover Kit's hand with her own.

"Let's go home."

Ivy, Kit and Callum sat around the foot of the stairs, lacing up their boots while they worked out their plan.

"The trouble is, I'm not sure exactly where the door was. I can't say for certain when I passed from our world into this one, and what if I can't find my way through again?" Kit said.

"There's no question of us splitting up," Ivy said firmly. "Whatever happens, we all need to go through the same door. Then we can work out what to do on the other side – however much time has passed – together."

Callum was concentrating on tying his laces, but he had a smile on his face that said he'd do whatever Ivy asked him to.

"It should be the hole in the wall, then," Kit agreed. "At the very least you two will be home, and I'm fairly sure I'll be able to find my way back to... to Mardale Green." Even the name of it sounded uncertain on his tongue now.

"We'll help you get there." Ivy finished her knot with a flourish and got to her feet. "Don't worry about that. We just need to work out the fastest route from here to Beckfoot. Callum, which way did you walk?"

Callum opened his mouth to speak, but Taliesin piped up from across the room, where he and Urien had remained sitting at the table, deep in conversation.

"Did I hear you say 'walk'? Don't you think you've done enough walking?"

"Never," Ivy replied curtly.

But Kit asked, "What do you suggest?"

"Well," said Urien, "there's a perfectly good train."

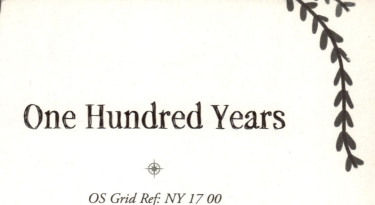

One Hundred Years

❖

OS Grid Ref: NY 17 00

That was how they came to find themselves standing at the edge of the train tracks, waiting in the grass. There wasn't a platform in sight, but Taliesin assured them it wouldn't be a problem.

"I thought I dredged the train line up when I remembered it?" Ivy asked.

"You did, but it comes and goes," Taliesin replied. "It sinks away when it's not in use, and when you need it... Aha! Here it is."

A far-off whistle echoed through the valley and a dull roar grew louder and louder. Ivy realised they were running out of time – there still seemed to be so much that remained unsaid. She turned to the fairy and the king.

"Thank you," she said. "Obviously we got off on the wrong foot, but... I just..." She couldn't seem to find the words to sum up their adventures and misadventures together, and the right way to say goodbye to it all.

Taliesin shook his head. "I think we're past all that,"

he said solemnly. "Consider all the thank yous and sorrys and goodbyes said and done."

Ivy couldn't dismiss the suspicion that this was particularly convenient for Taliesin, but it seemed like he and Urien had enough to deal with.

A green-and-black shape snaked out of the hills towards them. Taliesin held out his hand and Ivy shook it. When she extended her hand to Urien he clasped it in both of his and held on for a moment, smiling warmly at her. She couldn't help but smile back at the kindly expression on the face of the Spectre King.

Ivy's ears filled with noise as the great engine slowed and ground to a halt where they stood, belching out steam. The nearest door opened and a set of steps unfolded. Ivy, Grendel, Callum and Kit climbed into the carriage, closing the door behind them.

Inside there were booths with lacquered wooden tables, cushioned seats, and velvet curtains on the windows. A few other passengers were scattered around the carriage: two crossbill-winged fairy girls sitting and whispering together, a greying red fox staring out of the window, and a shepherdess at the back with three Herdwick sheep grazing the carpet at her feet.

They took their seats around a table, Grendel settling himself under Kit's legs. Callum gazed around the carriage in wonder, hands skimming every surface. As the train began to roll onwards, Ivy looked out of the window at the two men walking back through the grass towards the heart-shaped wood, hand in hand.

The ticket inspector strolled down the aisle towards them, a bronzed fairy covered in tattoos of trees. Their wings — a white-tailed sea eagle's — were almost too big to fit between the seats. "Where to?" they asked.

"Beckfoot?" Ivy asked hopefully. The fairy nodded, jotted down their destination, and moved on without asking for tickets.

Ivy watched the countryside speed by as the train chugged through the fells by no route she could understand. They travelled beneath the sheer scree of the mountains surrounding Wastwater, along the banks of peaceful Buttermere, through the quiet valley between Dent and Low Fell. She soaked in the kaleidoscope of colours in the seasonless trees, the abundant flowers and the glistening heliotrope surfaces of the lakes. Her chest constricted with a curious mixture of sadness to be leaving this strange, beautiful place behind, and a deep longing for home.

Occasionally the train stopped and one of the passengers disembarked at their destination, though there were no stations or platforms in sight. The fox got off at Ambleside, and the shepherdess guided her flock down the steps at Portinscale. No one else got on, and the inspector disappeared into the driver's booth.

After what might have been an hour Ivy realised that they were passing into the familiar landscape that surrounded her home village. Almost as if it sensed her recognition, the train began to brake. They gathered themselves together and clustered by the door until it came to a stop.

"Thank you!" Callum called as they jumped down.

The train had dropped them between the stream and the woodland that Ivy had entered on her first day in Underfell, hoping to find Callum in the trees, but stumbling upon Kit instead. Just on the other side of the beck was the hill that sloped upwards to the drystone wall. Even from here Ivy could see light – bright, true daylight – shining through the hole.

When the roar of the train had vanished into the distance, the air was still filled with rumbling as the train tracks were eaten again by the earth.

They crossed the beck one at a time, taking great reaching steps over the water. Grendel bounded across and led the way up the slope towards the garden wall.

Callum ran ahead, but Ivy walked side by side with Kit. It was so quiet now that the birds had stopped shouting at her all the time – she almost missed the reassuring chorus. The odd blackbird sang, but for the most part, the trees were still. Ivy noticed how quiet her companion had become and reached out to take his hand.

"Whatever… whenever it is when we get to the other side – however much time has passed – we'll face it together. The four of us," she said.

Kit squeezed her hand and met her eyes with a smile.

A shrill cry sliced through the air. All four of them looked up at once. The distinctive chequered wings and arched silhouette of an osprey soared through the violet not-sky above.

"Nessa!" Ivy laughed. Callum practically jumped out of his skin in excitement. But she wasn't the only bird in the sky. A platoon of Taliesin's hawfinches flitted here and there like a cascade of autumn leaves. A seagull announced itself with a laughing call, sailing over their heads in grey and white: Æthelred. Ivy gave a great wave to them all in farewell.

When they came to the wall Ivy ran her hands over the smooth old stones. Here in Underfell there was no village to be seen on the far side, no garden, no tilting grey slate house.

Callum, however, was not peering over the wall, but through it. "I see home!" he called excitedly.

"Wait!" Ivy cried. "One after the other, okay? We have to go through together."

"I'll go first," said Callum. "Ready?"

Suddenly Ivy was filled with uncertainty – it was happening too quickly. She turned to Kit. "I'll see you on the other side, all right?" she said, without projecting any of the reassurance she had intended.

Kit caught her by the arm when she tried to turn away. "Even with everything we've been through – I'm glad I was with you." He squashed her into a hug, his arms folded around her shoulders, and she squeezed his middle. But she let him go just as quickly, determined not to treat this like a goodbye. She couldn't bear the thought of Kit lost and alone again.

"GO!" Callum shouted, and launched himself through the hole.

Without a second to think, Ivy rushed through after Callum and stumbled out into the blinding sunshine on the other side, birds singing and lawnmowers whirring and children shouting in the distance. Callum was already rushing through the long summer grass, laughter erupting out of him.

Ivy turned back at once to the hole in the wall.

"Kit?" she called.

There was no answer.

Was he still on the other side? She peered between the stones and saw nothing but the rustling grass of the hillside in the lavender light, dotted with a few gold-splashed sheep.

"Kit!" she called again, louder this time. "Grendel?"

But there was no response.

He hadn't come through with them.

Ivy turned wildly to Callum, who had stopped gambolling about the garden like a lamb and was staring intently at a long, flat stone at the base of the wall.

"Callum," Ivy said helplessly, all the grey feelings of the past year rushing back to the surface, threatening to submerge her.

"Look," her little brother said. In a daze, she found her way to his side. But when her vision swam back into focus and she saw what had caught his eye, she dropped to the ground to take it in closer.

There were words carved into the stone, lichen growing in the cracks.

I + C
I'm home
Kit Kepple
1917

Tears sprang to Ivy's eyes at once. She blinked them back.

He was home, he was home, he was home. Her mind sang with it. He would see Mardale Green again. He would see his family again. He would mourn with them, and lay Billy to rest.

But there was a tiny hole in her relief that echoed with loss. *He's gone.*

"Callum! Ivy!"

A voice cut across the garden from the house – their mother's voice. Callum leapt to his feet and whirled around, tugging Ivy up with him. Iona stood in the doorway, waving. "Where have you two been all day?"

After dinner, although she felt tired enough to sleep for a month, Ivy went back outside with Callum and an armful of maps and walking guides. At the last moment, she snatched the fairy book from her window seat and added it to the collection.

Callum hopped over the garden wall into the field

beyond, sat down cross-legged in the grass and spread out a map in front of him, already shouting out ideas for new routes and camping trips they could take now that it was the summer holidays.

Ivy, meanwhile, walked slowly up to the garden wall. When she crouched down and peered through, she found that the hole was nothing more than a hole. She could see through to the field, the beck and the woodland on the other side, but there was nothing uncanny about it: no lilac tinge to the air, no mismatched flocks of nosy birds, only cloudless skies above.

Ivy climbed over into the field and zigzagged across it, flattening the grass into new paths leading in every direction. Eventually she plopped down on the ground beside Callum, digging through the stack of books until she found the green cloth-bound hardback with the golden writing: *Folk Tales and Fairy Places of Cumbria.*

She ran her fingers over the strange illustration etched on the front cover, of the higgledy-piggledy circle of shapes, one of them standing off to the side. And she realised, with a start, what she was looking at.

It was Long Meg, and all her daughters, as seen from above. A bird's-eye view.

Her heart stopped. She turned the cover to the frontispiece and looked for the first time at the name of the author.

Christopher Kepple.

Her mouth falling open, she flipped to the back of the

book, where a grainy black-and-white photo depicted a young man with untidy black curls, his arms wrapped around a border collie whose tongue was halfway to licking his cheek. The caption read:

The author as a young man
with his dog Grendel

Ivy let herself fall back, resting against the cushion of the springy grass beneath her. She let the cloudless blue sky fill her vision, bracing herself for the first rush of panic in her chest, for the grey fog to descend.

But all she felt was the fresh, familiar air tickling her face, and the faint scent of sheep on the breeze. She smiled so broadly that she started to laugh.

Callum was holding out the map, trying to show her something interesting he had found for them to do. "Let me see, then," she said, taking it from him. The two of them pored over the map together, beneath the wide blue sky.

THE END

Glossary

- **Beck** – a stream
- **Fell** – a mountain or large hill
- **Fell pony** – a hardy breed of pony native to the mountains and fells of Cumbria
- **Helm Wind** – a strong north-easterly wind over Cross Fell, Cumbria, and the only named wind in the UK
- **Lonning** – a lane
- **Nowt** – nothing
- **Owt** – anything
- **Rheged** – (pronounced *REG-ed*) the name of an ancient kingdom in the early Middle Ages which is believed to have incorporated much of Cumbria
- **Smit marks** – colourful marks painted on a sheep's fleece by farmers to identify their flocks
- **Tarn** – a small mountain lake
- **Tup** – a ram (a male sheep)
- **Yan, tyan, tethera…** – (pronounced *yan, tay-AN, TETH-era…*) a method of counting sheep used by shepherds in some areas of Britain (one, two, three…) from the extinct Cumbric language

About the Author

Alex Mullarky is a writer and veterinary nurse who loves creating stories about nature and magic. As a child she was happiest exploring imaginary worlds in the fields behind her home in Cumbria. Alex enjoys working with wildlife and has bottle-fed joeys in Australia and hiked with wild horses in the Rhodope Mountains of Bulgaria.

Alex lives near Edinburgh with four Australians (two cats, one dog, one human) and can be found wild swimming (sometimes with seals) and playing roller derby. *The Sky Beneath the Stone* is her debut novel.

You can follow Alex on Instagram at @saesteorra

Acknowledgements

Thank you to my wonderful agent, Zoë Plant, for believing in this story and putting in so much time and effort to transform the book. To the whole team at Floris Books, particularly my editor Jennie Skinner, who understood the magic straight away. It was a privilege to work on this book with a fellow Cumbrian.

The first drafts of this book were written on the lands of the Dja Dja Wurrung people. I pay my respects to Elders past and present, and recognise that sovereignty was never ceded.

Thank you to all the Screenies for making me feel at home when I was far away and helping me grow so much as a writer, particularly Meegan May, Jo Lourey and Diana Bick. To Kristen Proud for your time and support, and for running Squishy Minnie, my favourite bookshop in the world – and the Mules Book Club! And to my parents-in-law, for being early readers and enthusiastic supporters.

In the northern hemisphere, thank you to Karen Lee for always inspiring me to grow and explore. To Anna Coyle Taylor for your thoughtful feedback, and to Zoë Marriott for your kindness and guidance over the years. To Mairhi MacLeod for your beautiful photos and the stream of bookish content. To the Laurelbankers: this book was very much inspired by all your adventurous spirits. To Jess Meagher especially, mother of Æthelred.

Thank you to my grandparents for moving to Cumbria

and inspiring my parents to follow you. To my cousin Hannah for your insights, and to Naomie and Jenny as well, whose love and support for one another I have tried to reflect in the Norths. To my brothers, Conor and Jack, who explored Underfell with me when we were growing up. Thank you, Mum and Dad, for setting us loose in the countryside, for doing so much to enable us to pursue our dreams, and for always, always believing in me as a writer. I owe so much to all my friends and family.

Not only does it take a village to make a book, but much tradition, folklore and history also went into the telling of this story. I am grateful to all the books and websites that record these tales and from which I drew to create the world of Underfell. I hope that this story too will one day become blurred between fiction and folklore and be retold in many ways.

Thank you to all animal familiars past and present, for helping me feel at home in the world.

The final thank you is reserved for Laurel, who has effectively lived in Underfell with me for the past few years, whose spellworks include delicious meals and motivational Tizzie-Whizie sculptures. What can I say? You're the Urien to my Taliesin; here's to the next thousand years.